PREPPY

The Life & Death of Samuel Clearwater, Part Two

King Series, Book 6

T.M. FRAZIER

Print Edition

Samuel Clearwater, A.K.A. 'Preppy' finds himself back in a world he once loved, but no longer recognizes. His dim smile can't hide his inner turmoil and the people he views as family all suddenly feel like polite strangers.

Except for one person. A girl with dark eyes and even darker hair.

A girl who isn't even an option.

At least, not anymore.

Dre can't decide who she's going to listen to. Her heart, her head, or her body. Because two out of those three things have her heading right back to Logan's Beach. Closure is what she tells herself she's seeking, but when she unlocks doors that were never meant to be opened she soon discovers that when it comes to Samuel Clearwater, closure might NEVER be an option.

This is book six in the King Series and the second part of Preppy and Dre's three-part story.

Acknowledgements

As always, thank you to my readers. I'm stunned and humbled by your love and support for these characters and I hope to bring you many more that you'll love in the near future. LOVE to you ALWAYS!

Thank you to Ellie McLove, and Kim G. for making my words make a bit of sense. I'm not the best with all the grammar stuff, but you take what could be an epic mess and make it so the readers understand my crazy thoughts. I appreciate you more than you'll ever know.

Thank you to model Travis DesLaurier and photographer Corey Pollack for yet again providing me with an amazing picture to work with. This cover brings Preppy to life and seeing the image still gives me chills.

Thank you to Kimberly Brower, my agent who deals with my crap. I'm not easy to work with. I don't know what a deadline is and I am horrible with scheduling and organization, but having you in my corner makes this entire process less stressful. The fact that I can call you and vent when something is something I'll never take for granted. Thanks for taking a chance on me. I'll work hard to make sure you never regret it.

Thank you to my Frazierlanders! You bring me so much joy every single day.

And of course, thank you to my husband who loves and supports all my crazy, and our beautiful daughter who is truly the best gift we've ever received. Mommy loves you, baby girl! <3

Dedication

For Logan & Charley

Every man dies. Not every man really lives.

-William Wallace

Authors Note:

Dear fantabulous reader,

Preppy and Dre have a lot of story to tell. That's why I broke it up into parts. It's not just a love story between two people, it's a story about family, loyalty, and the kind of love that goes BEYOND romantic love.

For Preppy it's also about being thrown back into a world he hasn't been in for a long time and trying to find what his roll is now that everything has changed.

For Dre it's also about finding her way on her own and learning who she really is by learning what she really wants out of life.

I'm telling you all of this because not every scene is the two of them together. There is too much I wanted to tell you to just focus on the romance part of the story, and because you love Preppy so much I wanted to give you all of him, not just one side of him.

Don't worry, there is plenty of romance, but there is also so much more.

I love you all. Thank you so much for your support and for allowing me to live my dream. I hope you love Preppy Part Two as much as I've enjoyed writing it and I really look forward to bringing you the third part soon.

Love Always,
T.M. Frazier

PROLOGUE

PREPPY

THERE'S THIS LIGHT in the distance. It's bright, burning, and blinding as fucking hell. It's just out of my grasp. A whisper away. I can talk about it. I can think about it, but it's almost like it's not real. Like it's not really fucking there, and it drives me insane because all I can think about is reaching for it.

Reaching for you.

Because as my letter said, YOU are my light when I'm surrounded by nothing but dark.

I try to ignore it, the echoes of my name being called between time and space, because FUCK death.

Fuck anything that tries to keep me from finding my way back to you. If and when I'm liberated from the shackles that keep me tethered to the gates of hell, have no doubt, I'm coming for you, Doc.

Because YOU are what has kept me alive all these months.

Kept me WANTING to be alive.

Which is fucking hard sometimes because when death calls out to me, he sounds like an old friend offering comforts that would be so fucking easy to take. But you know me, probably better than anyone, and I've never been a man to take the easy route. Maybe that's why I've chosen instead to take the road back to you.

To the US.

The Reaper came for me, and he demanded that I take his hand and he told me he was my friend, my companion in death.

I couldn't help myself when I laughed in that fuckers face and told him his sister gives good head. Luckily he sent me right back across the river on my merry fucking way.

Back to LIFE.

Back to POSSIBILITY.

A long time ago, when I was just a skinny little nothing being beaten up by a bully in the school yard, I met someone who defended me when no one else would. We made a plan to be our own bosses that very day. It didn't matter that we were just kids because we meant it then, and I mean it just as much right fucking now.

Which is why, when faced with the fucking end of my life, I spit in the Reaper's face.

Because my name is Samuel Clearwater, and I take orders from no one.

Not even death

CHAPTER ONE

DRE

"WHAT DOES HE mean by that?" Ray asked, coming over to stand next to me at Preppy's bedside. After his sudden outburst he'd passed back out, leaving me more disoriented than when I walked in the door to find him ALIVE. "Why did he call you his wife?"

I shook my head. "I...I'm not really sure," I answered, not able to focus on her question, still consumed with the fact that Preppy was alive. Battered and looking nothing like his former self.

But ALIVE.

"It was probably just nonsense," Bear said from the doorway. "He's been muttering a bit over the past few days. One of the doctors thinks it's a sign that his body's healed enough to start fighting his way out of the coma. He said it might still be a few weeks, but it's a decent sign."

"Yeah, but those other two quacks think it could be just reflex's, and it don't mean shit," King added, looking every bit skeptical.

"How...how is this...how is this even possible?" I asked, covering my open mouth with my hand. I leaned over his body like I was checking to see if he was real or if my teary eyes were deceiving me. His chest rose and fell, and it sounded like the most beautiful music I'd ever heard.

Ray paused as she was about to answer like she was considering my presence with a new kind of skepticism. She stared hard at where my hand was touching Preppy. Apparently, she was the only one who questioned my intentions, because the other three that were with her had disappeared from the doorway, leaving the two of us in the room alone.

NOT alone.

With PREPPY.

I squeezed his hand and let out a sigh of relief, sending out a few thank you's into the universe along with a few choked sobs.

"He was…" Ray looked at the floor and shuffled her feet. She crossed her arms over her chest. "He was here the whole time. In Logan's Beach," she said, like she still couldn't believe it herself.

I gasped. "Why? How?"

"We don't know a lot of the details. Just that he was being held close by and that the guy who was holding him must have had a lot of people in his pocket to make us all believe he was dead."

"What did the police say?"

It dawned on me how stupid my question must have sounded when Ray cocked her head to the side. "How well did you know Preppy?"

"Well enough to know it was idiotic of me to ask about police involvement." I flashed her a tight-lipped smile.

Ray nodded as if I answered correctly. "King and Bear are on it. They're not trusting anyone to look into it but themselves. They've been up most nights until the sun comes up going over theories and retracing everyone's steps to find out who else could be involved." She pointed to Preppy, "But only he knows what happened down there, and there isn't any way a single second of it was something good. The only thing we know is that he's lucky to be alive. We are all so lucky that he's alive."

"Yes, yes we are," I agreed, turning my attentions back to Preppy whose eyebrows were pointing in toward the middle of his face in a sharp V as if he were having some a nightmare he couldn't escape.

"You said you were a friend of his?" Ray asked again like she needed more clarification than what I'd given her.

That makes two of us.

"We met a long time ago," I said, not knowing what the right answer was. I had no clue what we had been, only what we didn't become. "Preppy saved my life once," I told her for the sake of giving her something about my connection to Preppy. "more than once." I laughed and wiped a fallen tear from my cheek.

Preppy suddenly sat up with a startled roar, his arms shot out and before I could swallow down the frightened sob threatening to escape from my mouth his hands were wrapped tightly around my throat. Squeezing, squeezing, until I saw stars and my windpipe was closing under the power of his relentless hold.

The pressure behind my eyes was building until it felt like they were going to pop from my head. I felt the blood vessels exploding in anger under his relentless hold.

I couldn't even scream. Preppy pushed me roughly. My shoulder blades stung as I crashed into the wall. A colorful plastic clock fell from its nail and bounced off the top of my head before falling to the floor. An eerie rendition of 'someday my prince will come' played slowly from the clock as Preppy stared intensely into my eyes with all the chords in his neck taught and his teeth gnashed together. I search his eyes for some flash of recognition, but it wasn't there. I knew by the deadened look in his eyes that it wasn't me he saw, to him I wasn't even there. He squeezed my throat tighter. His hips pinned me in place. I grew weaker and weaker by the second. There was no fighting back. There was no way to win.

I was going to die, and if I could've laughed, at that moment I would've because my final thought was that at least I got to see Preppy before my death, even if he was the one killing me.

Using his grip around my throat as if his hand were a collar and his arm my leash, he lifted me off the wall and for a second I felt as if he were going to let me go.

Instead, he slammed me back, harder. This time it was a shelf of coloring books that rained down on us. There was shouting, an inaudible legion of voices both male and female, but they started to fade just as quickly as it came.

Suddenly, the pressure around my neck was gone, and I dropped to the floor, gasping for air I can't seem to find. The shallow breaths I did manage hurt like someone set fire to my throat. It was shitty breathing.

But at least I was breathing. My vision slowly returned and the voices that seemed so far away only moments ago were now right in front of me.

King and Bear had Preppy by the shoulders. They hauled him against the opposite wall toward the bed. He screamed, loud and awful. The sound shot right through me. It wasn't until they wrestled him back onto the bed when he spoke actual words. "Motherfuckers, get off me! I can't. I can't!" His screams turned into sobs, and I watched as his resistance slowly left his body. His eyes rolled back in his head, and his body went limp. After only a few seconds his chest began to rise and fall steadily, and he became a passed out pile of thin limbs hanging off the mattress.

The second I knew he was safe I darted from the room, my hands wrapped around my injured throat. I bolted out the front door, temporarily blinded by the sunlight, and by HIM.

"Wait!" Ray called from behind me, but I didn't stop. One foot in front of the other until I was in the car and speeding down the road at twice the legal limit.

I pulled over into the first parking lot I came across. A drug store. I killed the engine and dropped my head onto the steering wheel. Sobs escaped me. Cries of both relief and confusion erupted from me like a volcano of pent-up emotion. After sitting there in the car for what seemed like only minutes, I finally gathered myself together enough to be able to sit up straight and check the clock. Nope, not a few minutes.

A few hours.

I wiped the tears from my cheeks with my fingers. Then, out of nowhere, as if I had no control over my emotions or reactions, I started to laugh. Preppy...was alive.

He was *alive.*

My laugh grew louder. Manic. A high pitched cackle even I didn't recognize. The entire situation was unbelievable. Unreal even. Absurd. Surreal. Beautiful.

A fucking miracle.

So much for closure.

CHAPTER TWO

DRE

I STOOD ON MIRNA'S driveway and inhaled deeply, taking in all the smells that I'd missed over the past few years. The salty water from the Gulf of Mexico in the not too far distance, the oranges from the dozen or so groves one town over, and the mouth-watering scent of bar-b-que that I could practically taste in the air from a nearby roadside pit.

All the smells of Logan's Beach.

All the smells of home.

But it felt off. Like the sky shouldn't have been so blue. There shouldn't have been any picture perfect white fluffy clouds floating across it either. It felt wrong that stoplights still changed from red to green and back again, and that kids on rusted bikes chased the ice cream truck down the street, the broken speakers playing a haunting version of a typically upbeat tune.

Don't even get me started on the fucking church bells.

The funny thing about life is that even though something entirely earth-shattering rocks you to your core, something that shakes you off your access, the world around you somehow doesn't feel the impact.

Or it doesn't give a shit.

Meanwhile, there I stood, out in the blazing sunlight, on the most beautiful mid-summer day, waiting to be hit by the meteor that killed the dinosaurs. I was on edge, twitching like it hadn't been years since I gave into my heroin cravings. I loved everything about Logan's Beach but couldn't bring myself to enjoy it. Almost like I felt guilty that I could smell these amazing things while Preppy couldn't. Not now in that bed and probably not from wherever he'd been for the last year.

I had to put an end to my thoughts before they got ahead of me. Closing my eyes tightly, I shook off the thousands of bad things running through my mind.

Two little kids chose that moment to zip down the street laughing like rabid hyenas. One was on a bike, towing the other who was sitting on a skateboard. They reminded me of how much fun I used to have with my stepsister when I was younger.

I gave them my best mental middle finger.

Not because they deserved it off course, but because I had no idea how to put one foot in front of the other, and they were having the time of their lives.

Maybe I should hang out with them.

I guess it was a good thing the world went on, because if it paused to match what was going around inside of me, it would've looked a lot less like blue sky and bicycles, and a lot more like zombie and apocalypse.

Focus, Dre, I chastised myself. You have to focus. For dad.

"Hey, Dre, are you in there?" Brandon asked, waving his hand an inch in front of my face. "You totally zoned out on me."

I slapped it away, and he laughed. "Sorry, I'm a little preoccupied."

"We don't have to do this today," Brandon said. "It sounded

like what happened was rough. Anyone would be struggling right now; you don't have to..."

"No, I need to do this. I need to do something to occupy my mind, or I'll go crazy wondering about..." I paused, bouncing from foot to foot.

"Him," Brandon finished for me. He always knew what I was about to say and never let me get away with my instinct to keep things bottled up inside. "You're wondering where you go from here, right? Now that he's alive?" There was no judgment in his voice. Only concern.

I shook my head. "No, I mean, Yes?"

Brandon rolled his eyes and turned me by the shoulders to face him. He waved his fingers in a 'hit me with it' motion, and I knew he meant for me to continue because it was what he always did when I was stubborn with my words. I took a deep breath. "I thought that yes, I don't know where to go from here, but the truth is that I don't know if he's going to recover just yet, the doctors don't even know. So a part of me doesn't want to think of him as alive just yet because it could all change again..." my voice cracked, and my eyes fell to the gravel.

"Hey, look up here," Brandon said, taking my chin and directing my gaze back up at him. "Keep going."

"And even if he does..." I cleared my throat. "Survive? It doesn't change anything. He still drove me away. He still said things and did things to purposely hurt me, because he didn't want me."

"But he did want you. He wrote you that letter, and that was years after you left."

"Yes, but that was still a year ago now. And Preppy's been through god knows what life-changing situation. And even if all of that wasn't a factor, there is still one gigantic reason why we both know it wouldn't end with roses and sunshine, so can we please get back to talking about the house now?" I asked. Smiling in a ridiculously awkward way that exposed both my upper and lower teeth and made my face look like it got caught in a wind tunnel.

"Fine, but this isn't over, we're still going to talk about it," Brandon said, pinching my cheek to turn my face back to normal.

"Promise?" I asked, sarcastically.

"Smart ass," he mumbled. Brandon tipped his chin to the house. "You know, your dad didn't ask you to do this," he pointed out. "And I'm pretty sure he'd be pissed if he found out."

"Well then, we won't tell him now will we?"

"I thought part of your NA thing was no lies."

"It's not like I'm telling him I'm taking his car for a ride to the mall when in reality I'm planning to trade it to a chop-shop for a day's worth of dope. It's not like I'm even lying; I'm simply omitting the truth for his benefit, not to his detriment."

"Whatever lets you sleep at night," Brandon said, rolling his eyes dramatically. He pushed the sleeves of his button-down shirt up his forearms arms. "Be sure to run it by your sponsor, Andrea. I think she'll have something to say about the logic you've concocted on that one."

"You leave Edna out of this," I jokingly warned, wagging my finger at him.

I shielded my eyes from the sun as I turned from Brandon to look up lovingly up at someone else I love. Someone much older, showing a lot more wear-and-tear.

Mirna's house.

And because Preppy stuck to his word, MY house.

My heart skipped a beat like I was on a first date. Immediately, I spotted the lines on the front porch post where my grandfather used to mark my height as a kid, and the crooked light on the side of the house that became that way when I was testing out an archery set my grandma had gotten me for my birthday one year. I even loved the way all the trees in the front of the house leaned to the left, the result of a hurricane that hit the summer I was nine. My old friend was in need of some repair, having sat neglected for a few years, but she was still beautiful to me. She always would be.

Even if she won't be mine for much longer.

The step on the porch, the one I'd fixed before, was warped again. This time it was the other side curving upwards in a wing-like position as if it was about to take flight. The roof had lost a lot of shingles, leaving blotchy patches of faded tar paper peeking out from underneath.

The entire house was like another character in the story of my life.

An important one.

All through rehab, getting my GED, going to the local community college, I'd always had this idea. A plan to move to Logan's Beach permanently after I graduated. I'd fix up the house and make it a place I could be proud of in a town that I could never quite shake.

For better or worse, Logan's Beach was a part of me.

A place where my life almost ended, and where it almost just began.

However, if I'd learned anything about life post-rehab, it's that plans change, and you must learn to adapt. First order of adjusting: Sell the house to help dad.

"You've always talked about how much you love this place," Brandon said with his nose wrinkled as he looked it over, like he couldn't understand the appeal in a shaggy old cottage on a forgotten road in the middle of a little town with two street lights and three stop signs.

"I do love this place," I argued. "But I love my dad more. Selling it is the least I can do for him."

"Dre, it's not your fault that his business isn't doing great," Brandon pointed out. "He owns a bookstore when the world has shifted to buying books online through Bookazon dot com."

"I know, but it IS my fault he took out a second mortgage to send me to rehab and a personal loan to send me to school. He brought Mirna up to live by us in a facility that cost a lot more and took on all of her expenses because I wanted to be close to her in her final days. It's because of me that he's swimming in debt. I may not be the reason his business is failing, but I AM the reason he's losing his house," I said choking up when I thought about all the pain my addiction and my lies and my lack of giving a shit had caused him through the years.

Brandon raised an eyebrow at me and tucked his thumbs into his belt. He glanced at the house then back to me. Looking confused and out of place. Sweat stains formed around the collar of his white dress shirt, the material too thick for the wet heat of Southern Florida. The humidity caused his usually tame dark hair to jut out from his head at every available angle. His overly tanned skin stood out against his crisp white dress shirt which he pulled from the waistband of his pants, fanning it up and down to trap air underneath. If I watched him much longer, I was pretty sure he was going to melt right there on the driveway.

I walked over to the porch and tested the first warped step

with my sneaker, and it disintegrated into crumbles under the tiniest bit of pressure.

"My dad needs my help. He just WON'T ask for it. You know how stubborn he is; you used to work for him. Besides, he still sees me as a kid, as an addict, he doesn't want to put any pressure on me." I tested two more steps which held up slightly better than the one that turned to wood dust. "I think he's afraid of pushing me over the edge again." I hopped down the steps and walked over to the garage. I ran my hand over the single bay garage door, leaving a streak in the dust coating it. Remembering all the things my grandfather taught me inside that garage. Painting, welding, drilling.

"Your dad loves you," Brandon said as I joined him back on the porch. He followed my lead carefully up the steps, only placing his foot where mine had just proved we wouldn't go crashing down into the crawl space underneath.

"I know. And I love my dad. That's why I'm doing this. And if it wasn't for the past due notices I found shoved into a drawer in his kitchen and the lawsuit from the mortgage company in his desk, I still wouldn't know he was losing his house."

"But still. This house is special to you. You look like you're going to make out with it for fuck's sake," Brandon said with a laugh.

"I don't know about the making out part," I said, returning his smile. "But it is special to me. It always will be," I admitted, "But if I'd known earlier what dad was going through I would have sold it a lot sooner. He should never have…"

"Stop, Dre. You needed rehab. You needed to get your ass in school. Your dad did the right thing by you. He didn't tell you because he doesn't want you to worry. I thought you were done blaming yourself? Isn't that another one of your NA things?" Brandon tugged me into his side and gave me a quick kiss on the head before releasing me. Brandon and I didn't have any secrets. He knew all my dark and dirty, and I knew all of his, although cheating on a test in sixth grade is about as dark and dirty as Brandon had ever gotten.

"Thanks, Squeaky," I said, using my nickname for him. It stood for squeaky clean. "I'm always working on it."

I took my time opening the front door, remembering the way Mirna always used to be on the other side of it to greet me with a smile and her famous cookies. It felt wrong that she wasn't around. In the house, or in the world.

Mirna died six months earlier.

"Well, if you are adamant about this sale then I insist on helping you fix this place up," Brandon said, smoothing his brown hair back with both hands. He unbuttoned his shirt, revealing more sweat soaking the white tank top underneath. "What do you need me to do?"

I cocked an eyebrow at him. "You? Help? What do you know about fixing up a house?"

"Not a damn thing," he admitted with a laugh, his dark gray eyes lighting up with amusement. His big smile showed off more bright white teeth than should be able to fit in one mouth. "But you know about all this stuff, and you can teach me. I'm a quick learner. Besides, what did you think I came all the way down here for?"

"Because my dad asked you to babysit me," I answered honestly.

"No, for moral support and handyman services," Brandon said. I tried to contain my laugh. The last thing handy I saw

Brandon attempt was when he hung a picture. Within three minutes it fell off the wall.

I rehung it.

The house was going to need a lot of work to bring it up to sellable condition but time wasn't on my side. I could use any hand offered and right then, Brandon was the only hand offering. "Alright, Brandon, let's go then. I'm Tim the Tool-Man, and you're Al."

"Why do I have to be Al?" Brandon whined. "He wears plaid."

"More facial hair," I joked, but my smile quickly fell the second I entered the living room and a powerful sense of deja-vu I'd ever experienced slammed into me. Then the memories came back to me one by one like I was experiencing them all over again. Sitting in the living room trying to con my grandmother, running from a spray of Preppy's bullets into the woods, meditating with Mirna in the backyard, and sleeping with Preppy's body wrapped around mine in my little bed.

Chills danced up my spine.

Just as I got to the kitchen and another round of memories took shape in my mind a throat cleared from behind us. I jumped around to find Ray standing in the doorway. Her long blonde hair was stick-straight, the breeze blowing through the porch made it so she had to keep tucking the wayward strands behind her ears. She wore a simple white tank top and a pair of cut-off denim shorts. A baby, no more than six months old, bounced on Ray's hip, dressed in all pink. The little one shared the same bright blue eyes as Ray.

My heart squeezed when the baby giggled, pulling on a crown necklace Ray wore around her neck. "Hi, Ray, come on in," I said, and then my thoughts immediately went to Preppy.

"Is everything okay?" I tried not to let my sudden sense of panic seep into my voice.

"Yeah, everything's fine. I just wanted to come by and say that I'm sorry about what happened this morning with Preppy," Ray said, looking around the empty living room while bouncing the giggling baby.

"It's not your fault. It's nobody's fault," I said. "Wait, how did you know where I was?"

"Small town. Just gotta throw a rock in the right direction."

"Hi, I'm Brandon," Brandon said, introducing himself and extending his hand to Ray.

"Hi, so great to meet you, Brandon," Ray said. "I'm Ray and this here is little Nicole Grace."

"Awe, like after Grace, Grace?" I asked as Brandon and Ray shook hands.

Ray cocked her head to the side. "Yeah, like the one and only," she said, covering her suspicious reaction with another smile.

"Well nice to meet you, Nicole Grace," Brandon cooed in his best baby voice. He shook the baby's hand with his thumb.

"I'm so sorry. I should have introduced the two of you," I apologized. "I've just got a lot on my mind right now, and it seems that my manners didn't make the list."

"No worries," Ray said taking a stroll about the room, checking out the bare walls and low-hanging wood beams that ran across the ceiling. "I saw the for sale sign in the car. Is this your place? You're selling it?"

I nodded. "It used to be my grandmothers," I rocked back on my heels with my hands in my back pockets, happy to be back in the house, even if it was just for a short while.

"It's beautiful," Ray said, admiring the view of the backyard through the filthy kitchen window. Even though the place was in shambles, I believed her compliment was genuine, because she was looking around like she could see the house for the place it could be again, and not the place it was. "I'll keep my ears open, and if I hear about anyone who's looking to buy, I'll send them your way," she offered.

"Well then I'll give you the grand tour, so you know what you'll be sending them too," I said, leading the way down the hall. Ray followed close behind. "Although I will warn you. The house isn't super big, so it's going to be a very short tour." Ray laughed, and so did the baby.

"I'll go get the rest of the stuff out of the car," Brandon said, heading out the front door.

"My grandfather built this house," I said. "It's three bedrooms and two bathrooms although I know it doesn't look it from the outside." I opened the first hallway door. "This used to be my room." Ray peeked her head inside, and I shut the door again. There would be plenty of time for me to sit and stare at the strawberry wallpaper and faded yellow curtains and I didn't want to break out in tears in front of my guest.

"You used to live here, too?" Ray asked.

"Only during the summers when I was a kid. This visit is the first time I've been here in years though." I showed her the bathroom in the hallway and Mirna's old room before opening the door at the end of the hall. The mechanics of the former grow house might have been long gone, but the signs that it was once there were all around. The hooks in the ceiling. The nails in the walls where the pipes were connected.

"So that's how you know, Preppy," Ray lamented, taking a look around the room.

"Yeah, sort of," I admitted.

"When you came to the house, you really didn't know Preppy was alive, did you?" Ray asked.

"It was the shock of a lifetime," I admitted. "I still can't believe it." I closed the door and led us back out to the kitchen. I touched my hand to my throat, feeling the swollen markings left by Preppy's hands.

I opened the sliding glass door to the backyard. Between the boards of the faded wooden deck, weeds grew from underneath, creating huge gaps between the panels. The lawn where Mirna taught me to meditate was grown over, having merged with the field behind it at some point. A train whistled in the distance.

"Well," Ray said, mulling over my answer. She set the baby in front of her on the counter and smiled down at the adorable chubby-cheeked infant. "That was one hell of a tour."

I looked down at the baby who had stuck one of Ray's fingers in her mouth and was gnawing away on it with her gums. "May I?" I asked hesitatingly, holding out my arms.

"Oh, of course," Ray said, picking Nicole Grace off the counter and setting her in my arms. My chest constricted, and I felt as if I couldn't breathe. She was the most beautiful thing I'd ever seen.

"You must just stare at her all day long, right?" I asked as I cradled the little girl in my arms.

"Yes, her daddy too. We're tired, but it's totally worth it" Ray said. "They all are." She pushed back a tiny lock of baby-soft hair from Nicole's little head. "Do have any?"

I shook my head. "No. I learned a while back that I can't have kids."

"I'm sorry," Ray offered. She must have sensed that I didn't want to talk about it anymore because she quickly changed the subject.

"I've got a few errands to run now," Ray said. "But how about we get together later on this afternoon after I pick the kids up from school and drop them off with King? We can have ourselves some girl talk. I only have Thia, Bear's old lady and she's pregnant. I can't tell you how tired I am of talking about diaper genies and boppy pillows."

"That sounds great," I said.

"You need any help with all this?" Ray asked, looking around the house to the peeling wallpaper and cracked drywall. "King and Bear are about as handy, and they come, and Bear has an arsenal of guys that would be willing to help for as little as a few beers."

I reluctantly handed Ray back her baby and walked them out the open front door. Ray carefully navigated her way down the rickety front steps. I glanced over at my helper who was still struggling to get the FOR SALE sign out of the hatchback of the rental car. "You know, Ray. I might just take you up on that," I said with a smile that she returned.

"Good, cause that boy over there is cute and all, but he looks like the type that wouldn't know a hammer if it fell from a shelf and smacked him on top of the head."

"Unfortunately, that's very true," Brandon huffed, after finally freeing the sign. The collar and armpits of his dress shirt were saturated with dark circles of perspiration.

"Oh, shit, I almost forgot the main reason I stopped over. I swear these little ones give me the biggest case of mom-brain sometimes," Ray said, speed walking over to the old Ford truck parked on the edge of the lawn. She reached in through the open window of the passenger seat and returned with a folded piece of paper. "I was thinking about what Preppy said earlier? The thing about you being his wife?"

"It was just something he said in confusion," I repeated the same reasoning I'd given her that morning.

"No, I don't think that's it," Ray argued, unfolding the page and handing it to me. It was a photocopy of the marriage certificate I'd made for Preppy. I shook my head. "No, you don't understand. This paper is just something I made up. It's a fake. All the signatures. The witnesses. All forged," I explained, pulling the paper down from my face to find Ray staring back at me like she was not convinced. "It was something Preppy needed when he was trying to get custody of King's daughter; it's not even real. There was no wedding. No minister. No nothing. It's…not real," I repeated the same words in an effort to get my point across.

Ray tapped the spot on the lower right corner of the page over the official county stamp, one that would be a raised on the original. It wasn't something I put there.

Ray continued, "I got this copy from the County Clerk's office this morning," she said. "And according to them…it's very very real."

"Shit," I swore, turning the page around like it could tell me something more by inspecting the blank side. "That makes us…"

"In the eyes of the State of Florida? Married," Ray finished for me, flashing me a wink. "Congratulations, Dre. You're Mrs. Samuel Clearwater."

CHAPTER THREE

PREPPY

A THOUSAND HOPEFUL WHISPERS breathed over my body. Little bursts of air peppered my skin as someone gently lifted my arm and two fingers pressed firmly on the inside of my wrist. I was tucked and untucked in varies stages of cocooning, wrapped in unfamiliar softness. The air around me was fresh and light with none of the sticky dampness I'd become used to clinging to the inside of my throat and lungs, the kind of wet air that threatened to choke me with the thick stench of mildew and decay.

The sound of heavy rain pelting against a window overhead rang in my ear drums. A clap of thunder boomed, rattling my aching bones. A burst of bright lightning immediately followed, flashing in front of my closed eyelids as if it was somehow announcing my new semi-conscious state to the world.

Or maybe, just to me.

"Look, his eyes are fluttering again," A female voice stated. "This could be it." For a second I envisioned the dark haired girl with black eyes and red lips. The one I thought about so often I started to question if she was even ever real or just part of a fantasy I'd created to pass the time. But when the voice kept talking the image of my girl faded and recognition took hold.

Doe.

My adrenaline surged as well as the immediate need to get the fuck up and join the world around me, the world I'd missed with every cell of my fucking being and the one I never thought I'd have the pleasure of existing in again. It was like it was Friday night and all my friends were going out to do something balls to the walls amazing, and I had to stay home and hear all about it in the morning, feeling shitty and left out.

It was like an extended night out, except with ass rape and constant beatings. Either way, there was a lot of catching up to do. But then I remembered that all wasn't always what it seemed. I paused and took a brief second to remind myself that what I was feeling, the voice I was hearing, it could be a product of my imagination just like all the times before. That the likelihood of NO ONE being there when I opened my eyes, or that it would be the fucking devil himself, was much greater than the possibility it being my friend.

I could be dead. Or it could all be some sort of fucked up hallucination.

Someone squeezed my arm. If it was the devil, he had tiny hands and used moisturizer.

But it wasn't.

The gesture was gentle. Friendly. Reassuring.

Nope. Not the devil.

Although that simple touch felt as if all the bones in my fingers were being crushed, it was also the greatest fucking pain I'd ever experienced because it told me that it all might be real.

I tried to open my eyes but it was like prying apart a frozen sandwich with your bare hands. All I could see were colors dancing behind my lids like a light show taking place behind a screen.

When I attempted to speak I choked on my own saliva, and for what seemed like a span of forever, a stream of erratic coughs was the only response I could muster.

"Maybe he's not ready yet," an unfamiliar female voice chimed in. "He might just need more time."

"No," Doe argued. "I know he's coming around. I just know he is. I can feel it. He can hear us. It's different now." Her voice was confident, albeit desperate, like she was trying to convince herself as well as whoever it was she was talking to.

"Have you two considered the possibility that he's just being a fucking pussy?" King boomed. There was no mistaking his voice. The fucker sounded louder than thunder amongst a drizzle of rain. "Maybe he's fucking with us. I wouldn't put it past him. Shit he could have been up for days already but just wants us to wipe his ass some more."

"Shhhhhhhh!" Was the response. I wanted to smile. To laugh. But nothing I wanted to do, things that were easy before, was happening. What used to be a natural reflex, something I never had to so much as think about, was now a massive struggle to will my muddled brain and somewhat useless body to get together and make the SS Preppy functional again.

"Fuck that shit. I'm not gonna be quiet. This isn't a fucking library. We're hoping he wakes the fuck up, so let's wake him the fuck up! He likes the attention, you know that. Miss Priss over here isn't going to open his eyes and grace us with his presence until he knows he's got all of our fucking attention." There was a pause and then I felt King's breath on my forehead as he leaned in close. His shadow fell over the light as he spoke to me just inches from my nose. "We're all here. You can cut the shit now, Prep."

"Stop," I started, barely scratching out the word. The room

felt silent except for a few gasps. I felt like someone took a tiny sharp rake and ran in down the inside of my throat. I wet my lips with my tongue and started again. "St…"

King leaned in even closer until his chest was against mine. "What was that, Prep?" His facial hair bristled against the bridge of my nose.

"Stop…" My eyes finally cooperated and opened slightly, although it still felt as if they were being held together with superglue, prying them apart was like pulling my eyelashes out by the fucking roots.

I peered through a blurry slit and found myself staring at the top of King's dark head of hair. Motherfucker was trying to cuddle with me.

It was fucking adorable.

"Prep, try again. We can hear you, but we can't understand you. Speak louder," he demanded, enunciating each word as if I was deaf and dumb, the volume of his voice kept changing between a muted tone and a megaphone blast. He leaned down even closer until I was positive he was trying to lay down on my fucking face and his ear was against my lips.

"Stop…trying to make out with me," I finally managed to say. "I'm not into facial hair."

King stood straight and I felt the immediate relief that his body was no longer crushing me. He leaned over me with a satisfied shit eating grin on his ugly ass face. Doe was on his left with tears in her big icy blue eyes. The girl I didn't recognize was obscured from my view. She took a step back to allow King and Doe more space next to the bed.

"Took you fucking long enough," King said, looking like a proud parent whose kid just said it's first words.

"We've missed you," Doe added as my eyelids grew heavy again. It was a struggle to keep them open, but there was no way I was closing them so quickly after finally getting a look at two of the people I never thought I'd see again. "So much."

King tucked her into his side and kissed her on top of the head.

"Is there anything we can get you?" Doe asked, wiping the moisture from under her eye with her pinky.

"Yeah," I answered, turning my head to the side so I could see them better. A sensation like a million electrical wires misfiring at the same time sent jolts of pain down my spine. Before I could stop it I let out a strangled cry.

"What's wrong? Do you need the doctor? Tell me what you need, Prep," Doe demanded, sounding panicked. She placed a hand on my shoulder and it felt like she stuck a hot branding iron into my skin.

"No," I said, clearing my throat. "But there are some things I do need."

Doe darted from the room and came back seconds later with a mini pink Barbie notebook and matching pen. "Go ahead," she said. She turned the page of the notebook and clicked the back of the pen. It made a cheering sound.

King knowingly gazed down at me like he knew what I was up to. It was a great look. It told me that no matter how much time had passed; he still knew I was an asshole.

I was fucking *home.*

I kept my eyes trained on King while I dictated my list to Doe. "You ready?" I asked. She nodded.

"Okay, Imma need some blow, the good shit, not the kind you get from that dick over in Harper's Ridge. Strippers of course, no less than C-cups, and they have to be open to all things anal." I thought about it for a moment. "Okay, that would make them hookers. Scratch strippers and insert hookers. I need the blood of a virgin goat, three bottles of vintage of Mexican tequila with the worm still in tact." I glanced at Doe whose pen wasn't moving over the page. She raised her eyebrows and lowered her pen to glare at me over the multi-colored notebook. Tears streamed down her face.

"I've missed you so much," she sputtered, dropping the pen and Barbie book on the floor she threw her tiny body on top of mine in a long tight hug. She buried her face in my neck and I felt her hot tears burning against my skin as they poured from her eyes.

I ignored the blood curdling pain radiating from my muscles. I even resisted the urge to scream or even flinch, because I didn't want to scare her away. "Missed you too, kid," I whispered. We stayed there, wrapped in our one sided hug for a long while until King cleared his throat and Doe lifted her head from my neck and looked up at him. "He's back," she sniffled.

"Yeah, Pup. He's back," King agreed, sounding like there was a 'BUT' following that statement that he was holding back.

"I'm back," I muttered, "but King STILL thinks you hugged me too long and is now hoping I fall back into a coma soon because I got to feel your fantastic tits pressed up against me."

"Something like that," King said.

Doe rolled her eyes playfully as King pulled her off me.

"'Cause I'm a total catch right now. Nothing screams, come hop on my cock like a battered body and a coma." My throat was no longer as scratchy and it was becoming less painful to speak in longer sentences. "By the way, did your tits get bigger?" I asked

Doe. "'Cause I feel like they've gotten bigger." I narrowed my gaze on her tight yellow tank top. Yep, they were definitely bigger.

"Prep," King warned.

"There's a lot to tell you," Doe said, placing her hand over King's chest. "So much has happened since…" King put his hand over hers.

"Before you guys say anything else, I'm going to suggest an edit," I said.

"A what?" King asked.

I held up a finger. "Just follow me for a second. Instead of tip-toeing around the subject by saying when I 'was gone' and instead of stating the obvious, like referring to it as 'that time I was held against my will and tortured to the verge of death over and over again at the hands of a psychopath', I'm recommending we switch it up a tad bit."

"Okaaay…"

"As much as I'd never like to think or speak of it again it's just not fucking realistic. And since it's fucking impossible to just NOT talk about it when so much of what is going on in my life right has to do with shit that happened while I was…in Narnia."

"You've got to be fucking kidding me. You want us to refer to your time in a hole under the MC as Narnia?"

"Yep, that's what I said."

King started to mumble which made me realize that someone was missing, a very big very shirtless someone.

"Where the fuck is Bear?" I made a move to sit up but my wrists were unable to support my weight to successfully make the transition. King bent over and lifted me up under my armpits, adjusting me into a much more comfortable slightly reclined position.

Neither King nor Doe answered my question. Instead, they looked at each other like they were having some sort of telepathic unspoken conversation that I wasn't to have any part of.

"What?" I asked, "I mean, where the fuck could Bear be that's more important? Unless of course he's out getting the hookers and blow, in which case, I might make a small exception."

"I'm right here, motherfucker," Bear grumbled as he came into view, standing on the other side of Doe. I didn't know if he'd been there the entire time or if he's just arrived. Either way one thing was clear to me right off the bat.

"All this time…" I said. "And you still couldn't find a motherfucking shirt?"

Bear snickered and placed his hand over my forearm in the same way he always shook hands with the bikers in his club. "Welcome back, brother."

Doe and King shifted over to grant Bear more access to me. He knelt down and leaned over the bed. I missed the easy launch of insults between us. I missed everything about the stupid fucker, even that stupid quirky smile the chicks always seemed to dig. Even the way he looked as if he was always pissed even if he wasn't.

Although a LOT of the times he was.

I opened my eyes as wide as I could and took in my old friend's appearance for the first time in god knows how long. He looked exactly how I remembered physically, blond hair, matching blond beard, tattoos, bright blue eyes, freckles, leather cut.

But in another way he looked different.

VERY different.

Happier, maybe?

No fucking way…

Seeing Bear happy was as likely as spotting a yeti in the backyard. Something I had to see to believe.

I couldn't dwell on the notion for too long because in a fraction of a second it all started to change. Bear's face morphed like a Dali painting. My smile faded from my lips as the image of my friend melted away and became something else.

SOMEONE else.

It was no longer Bear smiling down at me, happy to see his long lost friend. No, it was someone with deeper lines on his forehead and a permanent scowl on his lips. Someone who's blond hair had changed to gray and whose freckles had faded with time. His blue eyes were no longer bright and held no signs of loyalty or brotherhood behind him.

No sign of life at all.

Bear was gone and pure fucking evil was in his place.

Blood curdling screams filled the small room, echoing off the walls and through my ears, the familiar and fucking terrifying sounds of someone being brutally tortured.

My vision blurred and I faded back into the purgatory, grateful for the escape.

It wasn't until I was fully back into oblivion when I realized that those screams were mine.

CHAPTER FOUR

PREPPY

THE DARK CLOUDS around my thoughts started to clear. Each time I woke up the horror of what happened and the reality of where I was, separated more and more from one another until I finally realized what my friends were telling me was the truth.

I was free.

I was safe.

I was fucking ALIVE.

And best of all?

Chop was fucking dead.

The only thing that pissed me off was that I wasn't the one to end the cocksucker myself.

The good news was that I was starting to regain some of my strength. The pains in my muscle and bones turned from sharp stabs to dull aches.

The gunshot wound Chop never allowed to fully heal was finally closed, although very fucking angry looking. The skin around it was all twisted up into a kaleidoscope of distorted tattoos around a huge red hurricane shaped scar.

I called it the hurricane of hurt.

I hated what it did to my tattoos, but that massive ugly thing was gonna earn me a shit ton of street cred.

While my body was getting it's shit together, Doe and King took turns filling me in on the headlines of their lives. All the shit I'd missed like King finally getting custody of Max. I felt as if I was in an episode of Days of our Lives when Doe told me that she had a son who King had adopted, then they had a new baby, AND she finally had her memory back. I was positive they skimmed down on the details of the story, but I was happy with the cliff notes for the time being. And if I really needed to catch up on more details I could just turn on the TV around 2pm because I'm sure their story line was being played out on one of the daytime channels.

"So wait, I've been calling you, Doe…but what the fuck is your name?" I asked, pushing off the bed into a standing position.

"Ramie, but I go by Ray."

"Wow," I said. I knew her name wasn't really Doe but for some reason the thought of her having a real name was still a shock.

"You can call me, Doe if you want though," she said, and I felt as if she genuinely meant it. "I feel like I have a thousand names now, Doe, Raemi, Pup. Although Mommy is kind of my current favorite."

"Mine too," King added.

And as if they could sense that she was speaking about them, two little blonde kids appeared in the doorway. "Mommy, Mommy, Mommy, Mom, Mammmmaaaaaa," they both called, not waiting for her to answer, just continuously repeating her name just to make sure neither of their parents kept full control of their sanity.

"I take that back," Doe amended with a smile.

King ran and scooped both kids up into his arms. They kicked their legs and squealed in delight. "Come on you two, let's get you some lunch. And don't wake up your little sister or your mom will..." his voice faded as he stomped down the hallway.

"Where the fuck is Bear?" I asked, sitting up. He's the only one I hadn't seen much of. "I vaguely remember him being here when I first woke up." I bent my knees, testing the limits of my joints. Everything cracked and snapped and popped like a god damned cereal commercial, but it felt good to be standing on my own power.

Doe busied herself by fluffing the pillows. "Bear sat with you a lot, he's just been really busy at the club I'm sure. There's been a lot going on over there since he took the reigns."

"You mean since Bear killed Chop," I said. "It's okay, you can say his name. You said the fuckers dead now, right? Doesn't matter anymore."

If only that were true.

"Something like that."

"I wish I could have been there to see that," I said, shuffling my feet on the carpet and grabbing what furniture I could as I put more and more space between myself and the bed.

"Revenge isn't everything, Preppy. All that matters is that you're here."

"No, I don't wish that I was there to see Chop being killed as long as it happened. I wish I was there to see Bear getting a girl," I said and Doe laughed. "She must be something else. What's her name again?"

"Thia," Doe admitted. "You'll like her."

"I'm sure I will," I said, curious as to what the girl was like who made Bear want more than just a quick fuck.

Because if she's anything like the girl who made you want more…

Doe snapped me out from my thought. "I've brought you some clothes," she said, diverting her eyes from the back of my hospital style gown which I knew was open in the back because I felt the cool air from the A/C against my ass cheeks. "Are you sure you don't need any help?" she asked again.

"Nah. I just want to get dressed on my own. Feel human again. You know, one small step for mankind and shit."

"Prep," King warned suddenly appearing back in the doorway, this time minus the kids.

"Seriously, boss-man? I'm back from the dead and you're still gonna give me shit about Doe? I mean, in a situation like this, one pity fuck wouldn't be completely unheard of." I pointed out, fully prepared for King to sling my words right back at me.

"You can do and say whatever you want, Prep," King responded, in a surprisingly calm tone. Apparently, I wasn't the only one confused by his newfound zen attitude because Doe looked just as confused as I did. Then King smiled and it was then I KNEW something wasn't right.

Or maybe things have changed more than they've let on…

"Uh…I can?" I asked, my knees cracking as they began to work again. Slowly I shook the leg out and muscle memory took over I was able to take a few small steps. "What's the catch?"

"You can talk as much shit as you want to me as long as you're prepared to be dead again," he said, pulling Doe tightly into his side. "For real this time."

I scowled. "You're not a friend. You're a monster!" I cried dramatically, taking larger and larger steps as I crossed the room.

Suddenly, while doing my Preppy shuffle across the pink carpet, I was hit with a flash of memory.

My hands around a throat. Feminine screaming. Flashes of dark hair.

I paused.

"Was anyone else here besides you guys? When I woke up or maybe even before?" I asked.

"Were you expecting someone?" King asked.

"No, but I've just got this weird feeling…" I trailed off, staring at the shade of bubblegum pink on the wall. Although it was now pink, it used to be blue. My old room. The room where I broke down and wrapped my hands around Doc's throat. It must have just been a memory. A distorted one, but a memory at that. "Never mind. I think my brain is still misfiring."

Doe sat the clothes down on the bed.

"We'll be in the living room when you're done. You need help down the stairs?" King asked.

"Fuck off," I said, giving him the middle finger, which he returned.

"Welcome home, motherfucker," he grumbled, unable to hide his smile. It was like our version of hugging it out.

I love that big mean bastard.

I stared down at the clothes on the bed. A pressed white shirt, khakis, matching pink and yellow suspenders, and bow tie. It was my usual pre Narnia attire. I ran my hand down the soft clean fabric but when I picked up the shirt from the pile I dropped it back onto the bed as if it stung my hand. I pushed the suspenders and bow tie off the pile and rummaged underneath, opting for a pair of grey sweatpants and plain white t-shirt on the bottom of the stack.

I made my way out into the living room, holding onto the railing as I slowly descended the steps, each one becoming easier and easier as my muscles adjusted to the feeling of walking and I remembered how to put one foot in front of the other again.

Voices speaking in hushed tones stopped me before I turned the corner.

"I don't know why we lied to him, that was stupid," Doe said.

I could hear the guilt in King's voice when he responded. "What were we supposed to say? Yeah, Prep, you had a visitor while you were in a coma, and by the way, I don't know who that girl is to you, but you woke up in a panic, almost strangled her to death, and you called her your wife. Also, you kind of freaked the fuck out on Bear and we're guessing it's because he looks so much like his psycho old man so he's decided not to come around so you don't flip your shit and try to kill him again?"

My entire body stiffened.

She WAS here.

King sighed heavily. I peeked around the corner and his head was in his hands. Doe was rubbing his back, sitting on the armrest of the couch. The two kids were sitting at the table off to the side, picking the crust off their sandwiches and throwing them at one another.

"I know it's hard, but we have to tell him the truth. He deserves that much. We're his family. We can't lie to him."

"As his family it's our job to protect him, so we can't just dump all this shit onto shoulders at once either," King said. "He's already been through too fucking much. I just wish I would have known where he was. He was so close the entire fucking time. So fucking close..." King's voice trailed off.

I stepped out into the living room, ready to tell him that it wasn't his fault and he shouldn't blame himself for not knowing where I was when I real

She WAS really there.

Neither King nor Doe saw me limping into the room. King continued. "I mean, this shits, fucked up. How the hell are we supposed to tell him that Grace died?"

It was the shock shooting through my system that made me walk right into the coffee table and make myself known.

"Shit," King swore. He stood up and came toward me. I held up my hands and took a step back.

"We didn't mean for you to find out…" He started, running a frustrated hand over his hair. "It's my fucking fault."

"No, No," I said, waving them off and trying to keep down the bile rising in my throat. My legs again grew shaky but I stood straighter, not wanting to make them feel worse by breaking down in front of them. "You guys have nothing to feel guilty about. Grace was sick right? For a long time. I mean, I kind of already figured," I lied. I was positive Grace would outlive the cockroaches of the apocalypse. She could have been run over by a mac truck and I would've put money on the truck having more damage than her.

I turned back toward my room. Or what USED to be my room. "I'm just gonna go take a shower," I said heading back up the stairs.

"Preppy, wait," King called out but I kept going.

"He needs some time," Doe said.

With each step back to my room the threat of losing my shit grew greater and greater. It wasn't until I was behind the closed door when I let the tears fall.

And fall they did.

I cried for the loss of Grace, my mother in all ways except blood. The mother who never let me down. The woman who would let me have it when I'd done something she didn't approve of, but who wasn't judgmental. She loved me for me. She loved all my crazy.

She never tried to change me.

I never even got to say good-bye.

I eventually made my way into the shower, spending several minutes under the water long after it turned cold. When I finally dragged myself out I went to take a piss and caught a glimpse of my reflection out of the corner of my eye. I turned toward the mirror and faced someone I hadn't seen in a very long fucking time. Someone I used to like looking at.

A lot.

I wasn't fucking stupid. I knew that after the shit I'd been through that I wouldn't exactly be GQ material.

But I also didn't expect to be staring at a total fucking stranger either.

I leaned in close to the mirror. I felt around my long knotted beard with my fingertips and almost lost my shit when they dropped into my severely sunken cheeks. The bones around my dark and hollowed eye sockets protruded out like a fucking caveman. My once hazel eyes which now looked more like a muted shit-colored brown.

At least Grace won't ever have to see me this way.

Even when my hair was at its longest, I'd always kept the top long and shaved the sides to show off the tattoos on both sides of my head. Post-torture, the parts that were normally short were grown out well past my shoulders, and for some reason looked much darker than the medium blond I remember it being.

I looked like a skinnier, demented version of Jesus Christ.

Walking death.

I could count my ribs, something I hadn't been able to do since I was a kid and suddenly I was back on the playground again, getting the shit beat out of me by a sumo wrestler of a twelve-year-old who entered puberty well before his time.

Everything about the pathetic soul in that mirror told a story that didn't bare repeating. My head spun. I grabbed onto the sink for support and lowered my head, staring at the thin ring of rust around the drain.

After every single motherfucking thing I'd been through in my life, I'd never considered myself a victim.

But a victim was all I saw in that mirror.

With one last scowl at my reflection I shuffled over to the toilet and leaned on the wall, pulling out my flaccid cock to take the piss I'd started to take earlier, but I couldn't help but keep thinking about Grace.

You are a good person, my Samuel. You're a good boy. Grace's words rang in my head. *You are loved.*

Mid-piss I stepped away from the toilet, spraying urine on the seat and floor. I ripped open the cabinet under the sink. I knelt and my knees crunched loudly, like gravel being rubbed together. I groaned at the odd sensation and the even more awful sound.

"Are you okay in there, Preppy?" Doe asked from the other side of the door.

"Fine," I barked back. Of all people she didn't deserve my irritation. I instantly felt guilty. "Fine," I repeated, softening my tone as much as I could although it wasn't much when my teeth were still gritted and I was speaking through the splitting pain burning in my legs and torso.

"Okay, we'll all be out in the living room. So...you know. That's where we will all be when you're done. Waiting for you." Sadness filled her voice. "I'm so sorry, Prep," she added. I heard the slide of her hand as she ran it down the outside of the door followed by the light padding of her feet on the carpet and finally, the sound of the outer door of the bedroom clicking shut.

I reminded myself to apologize to her for being such a dick. She didn't deserve me throwing a tantrum just because of what I'd been through.

I was just so fucking tired. Tired of laying there in that bed for so long. Tired of wasting fucking time. Tired of not living.

Tired of being fucking dead.

And maybe I was just tired of being fucking tired.

Once I found what I was looking for I held onto the sink and righted myself to stand back up. I plugged in what I thought was the solution to my problem, waving it in the air tauntingly. "Bye-Bye, motherfucker," I said to my reflection. I flipped the switch and swear I saw panic flash in his eyes as the buzzing sound echoed off the walls of the small bathroom.

I clicked over to the shave setting and ran the clippers over the top of my head from front to back in one long stroke.

A sense of immediate satisfaction coursed through me as I ran my fingertips over the newly sheared section of my head.

I needed to do more.

Much more.

ALL OF IT HAD TO GO.

I didn't bother to cut the hair with scissors first so every strip

I shaved off burned like I was slowly being scalped, but I didn't stop. I didn't give a shit about the pain.

Not anymore.

Pain wasn't exactly a new thing for me.

However, freedom was.

Feeling free from the anger. From the regret. Free from not caring if I could ever be the person I was before all the shit went down.

That person was almost as much of a stranger as the fucked up Jesus in the mirror who was in the process doing some long overdue and much needed manscaping.

My head was bloodied and scraped as I worked the clippers over my head again and again.

I didn't fucking care.

More and more hair dropped down and piled on top of my feet. First from my head and then from my face when I started on my beard, until I was completely clean and skin that hadn't seen the light of day in years was now bared to the world.

To me.

The satisfaction I felt while cutting it all off quickly turned to disappointment and a sudden sinking feeling. I gripped the sides of the sink and let my head fall with a growl.

I'd expected to be staring at someone new.

Someone clean.

The reality was that I was anything but.

Rage burned in my chest, bubbling over to a boil when I realized it was still the tortured looking man from moments before.

Just clean shaven.

And now all the weight loss and scars were on full fucking display. Every lump and poorly healed cut. My once colorful tattoos on the sides of my head were tattered and scarred like tears in my paper thin skin, matching the many many ruined ones on the rest of my body.

A roar tore from my throat. I reared back and punched my reflection, sending shards of glass to the floor, dying the piles of hair with drops of thick red which also dripped down the center of the cracked mirror. It wasn't enough. I punched it over and over again, my fist burning with the pain of each impact against the glass. "I fucking hate you!" I screamed at the top of my lungs, spit flew from my mouth as I wailed and wailed on the mirror until my knuckles were completely covered in red.

I fell to the floor as my shoulders shook with rage turned despair. I crumpled into a ball, pulling my knees up to my chest and willed the world to go the fuck away.

Willing it ALL to go the fuck away.

I clutched my bleeding hand and went to the only place I felt safe. Deep in my mind to memories so clear and bright I thought sometimes that they'd never happened at all.

I closed my eyes and started to drift away amongst the piles of my stripped identity. I was so far gone down the path that took me to that place that when I heard all of the commotion going on around me, I couldn't bring myself to lift my head to see what it was all about. Not even when the door burst open, the hinges falling from the frame, skidding across the floor. Not even as a cascade of concerned voices, both male and female, shouted above me to one another.

Or maybe to me.

I couldn't even bring myself to open my eyes when I was carried from the room and placed back in the bed I'd grown to fucking hate because I was already there. Chasing after a girl with dark doll like eyes, raven black hair, and fuck-me bright red lips.

"Keep me," she whispers, crooking her finger at me.

I felt myself being turned over and inspected for more serious damage I might have inflicted on myself but I just let it happen because that didn't matter anymore.

Nothing did.

I chase her further and further until the voices around me faded away.

But no matter how fast I run, she just runs faster.

Soon I'm not chasing her at all anymore. She's gone.

I'm alone, standing on the train tracks. Unmoving.

Staring into the blinding yellow headlight of a train as it grows closer and closer…until it's too fucking late.

CHAPTER FIVE

DRE

I WAS MORE AWAKE than a college kid with a seven-cup-a-day Starbucks habit.

It was the middle of the night and after a very long day of fighting against the jungle like back yard, armed with a rented weed-whacker and a borrowed lawn mower, I should've been dead to the world, but no matter how much I tossed and turned I couldn't reach any sort of restful state.

Not that night. Not any night since I'd been back in Logan's Beach.

The moon glowed orange through the dirt caked windows. Tired of battling with the sandman I decided that sleep and I were going to have to break up for the time being.

I felt around for my glasses and put them on while I sat up with my back against the wall. I powered on my laptop while listening to the overgrown tree branches in desperate needed a trim, rustling against the roof. I fished a cherry sucker out of my bag and plucked the plastic off the top. Sucking on candy was a weird little trick I'd picked up in rehab that I used whenever I was feeling restless and that night I felt as if I was gonna jump out of my own skin.

With the house being empty of all furniture the usual creaks and groans from years past sounded as if someone were slowly walking around inside on the hardwood floors, each little noise echoing through the tiny rooms. Brandon was sound asleep in the sleeping bag next to me, lightly snoring in a way that made me think it was adorable, and also want to kick some of his perfect teeth in at the same time.

I clicked over to the local BY OWNER real estate website and decided to turn my sleepless night into a productive one by scanning the comparable sales in the area to see what else I could do in order to get the most money out of the sale that didn't cost a fortune. With each stroke of the keys and click of the mouse the thought of selling the house grew from a nagging in the back of my head that told me it was wrong to a sickening thought of how I was going to live with myself after it was all said and done.

You don't have a choice, Dre.

A noise in the kitchen, like something had fallen caught my attention.

I snapped my laptop shut and looked around the dark room, my eyes taking a moment to focus in the black space after staring at the bright screen.

I was used to hearing things at night. Being paranoid and exaggerating sounds in my head wasn't exactly new for me. I looked over to Brandon who was still sound asleep and realized it was probably nothing.

Finishing my sucker I reached into my bag for another but realized that I'd left them in my purse in the other room. Slowly I shifted out of my sleeping bag and tip-toed into down the hall trying not to cause too many more creaks on the floor so Brandon wouldn't wake up.

It was then I saw it. A tall thin figure standing at the screen door. I opened my mouth to scream but no sound came out. At the same time a flash of heat lightning lit up the backyard and for a brief instant I was able to make out the man wearing a black hoodie with the hood up.

My knees buckled when the recognition hit me and fell forward onto the counte top for support.

PREPPY.

The facial hair was gone, his face sunken in, but it wouldn't of mattered if he were standing there with a ski mask covering his entire face.

I would know him anywhere.

I pushed off the counter and darted for the door, throwing it open with such force it banged loudly as it crashed against the stopper. I stepped out onto the porch but I was too late. It was empty.

I reached inside and hit the switch for the back light. It flipped on just in time for me to catch the rustling of the trees just beyond the fence.

With my adrenaline racing I slipped my feet into my grass stained KEDS that I'd left by the door and took the porch steps two at a time. The latch on the fence gate was rusted and overgrown with weeds. It wouldn't give when I tried to open it so instead I climbed over the small metal fence, it rattled and wobbled under my weight as I jumped down on the other side.

The moon overhead was bright as hell and my only guide as I sprinted through the dark woods. I couldn't help but remember that the last time I was running in those very woods I was running away from the man I was now heading toward.

When I reached the clearing at the end and burst out from

under the canopy the water tower came into view, bathed in the full moon's light. I knew where I was going. Last time I was up there I was trying to end it all.

This time I had no fucking clue what was in store for me.

But I was determined to find out.

* * *

PREPPY

FOR THE FIRST time in forever I was outside in the crisp clean night air in the town I'd lived in and loved my entire life. The sky above me was cloudless and littered with a million twinkling stars.

It was the usual 80-plus degrees. Hot as fuck, but with a cool breeze rolling off the bay waters, taming down the humidity that always threatened to make your shirt stick to your skin in South Florida.

It was a beautiful night. Perfect in every single fucking way.

The kind of day that people up north only dreamed of.

It was a tropical paradise some wait their entire lives to experience.

And I fucking hated it.

ALL. OF. IT.

It was too fucking bright even though it was night. The moon too fucking high. The sky too cloudless. The air too clean.

I'm pretty sure there is a special place in hell for people that cursed a beautiful night like that one.

Didn't matter to me. I'd already been there.

Even the chirping birds flying overhead seemed so loud that at one point when I'd been climbing up the tower I had to cover my ear with one of my hands thinking that I was under attack.

It was like sitting in a surround sound theater and having seats next to the speaker during a screening of Alfred Hitchcock's, The Birds.

The familiar light scent of saltwater wafted into the air. I used to inhale it like a drug that could get me high, but now it made my stomach roll and lurch to the point where I had to clutch my stomach to prevent the rising bile in my throat from spewing out, all because of the stench determined to invade all my senses.

The world I came back to was a spinning ferris wheel of sounds and light, assaulting me at every turn and I was helpless to make it stop, when all I wanted was to get off the fucking ride I never signed up to be on.

Logan's Beach used to be *my* place. *My* security blanket. But coming out of the dark and into the blinding light I'd been craving for so fucking long wasn't at all what I thought it would be.

It was a new kind of hell.

I was *finally* home, and all I wanted was a piece of normality. Well, normal for me. But being there, looking down at the only town that had ever been home to me, I felt anything but normal.

And anything but at home.

It was right then. In that very moment. While inhaling the clean air I once thrived on that now made me want to vomit. While listening to the familiar sounds that used to give me peace, but now echoed through my brain like jack hammers on pavement. It was right then I knew I would never find the kind of normal I used to know. The peace I once had.

Not there.

Never again.

My only hope was to find a new kind of normal, but to me

that thought was scarier than any kind of torture I'd faced at the hands of Chop.

Which might explain why I'd sought her out.

Although the truth was I had no idea why I went to see her. Fuck, I didn't even know if she'd be there. But once the shock of Grace's death started to set in I remembered that Doe said Dre had been at the house and it kept playing those words over and over again in my head on repeat.

By the time I realized what I was doing I'd already snuck out in the middle of the night like some kid breaking curfew. Remembering that the window over the kitchen sink had a broken lock it wasn't too hard to shimmy the window open and crawl inside.

The house was dark. Quiet.

Empty.

Yet the second my feet hit the floor I knew she was there.

I FELT her.

All the doors in the hall were shut except for the room at the end the one that used to be the grow room. It was open but just a crack. Just enough to see the back of her head poking out of a sleeping bag along the wall beneath the back window. I wanted to see more of her so I'd opened the door slowly and was about to step into the room when she sighed heavily. That's when I realized she was awake. Slowly I stepped back out of the room until I was in the safety of the kitchen. I pulled myself up on the counter and crawled out the window I'd came.

I was on the porch about to leave when I saw motion in the corner of my eye. That's when I turned and saw her for the first time in what seemed like a lifetime.

I don't know what I expected if and when I ever saw her

again. But I certainly didn't expect to feel like all the wind was stolen from my lungs.

She wore a plain white t-shirt just long enough to make me wonder if she was wearing shorts underneath, the hem brushing the tops of her thighs as she walked. Her shiny black hair was pulled into a high ponytail on top of her head. Against the moonlight it looked so dark it appeared almost blue, like the feathers of a black bird. I'd never seen her wear glasses before but she wore thick dark frames around her dark eyelashes that she pushed up the bridge of her nose as she shuffled into the kitchen.

I couldn't move. I couldn't bring myself to do anything but wonder again why the fuck I was even there in the first place and stand there like an asshole, gawking at the most beautiful fucking girl I'd ever seen. Even more beautiful than I remembered. More EVERYTHING than I remembered.

A flash of lightning in the sky caught her attention and that's when her attention shifted to the door and she spotted me. Our eyes locked. My aching heart pounded against my chest and my every instinct screamed, *go to her.*

And I was going to. My brain had already sent the message to my leg to move and take that first step and I was about to when a flash of lightening interrupted my thought and instead I turned and darted back the way I came. Over the fence and through the woods when I realized that I couldn't.

I wanted to. I wanted to with every fiber of my white trash being.

I just fucking COULDN'T.

That's when my feet moved on their own accord and I found myself perched on top of the world I once conquered, wondering if I'd ever feel normal again when the platform rattled.

My neck snapped to the ladder that shook as if someone were climbing it. A set of feminine hands appeared, reaching up and gripping the handrail. It wasn't until she was fully up on the platform, dusting herself off. Her dark hair blowing all around her face that she finally spoke. "You know, if you're looking for a place to jump from, someone once told me that The Causeway has a mostly five-star rating on Yelp for best places in Logan's Beach to end it all."

CHAPTER SIX

DRE

"Doc," Preppy acknowledged. I knew he was there yet nothing could've prepared me for the impact of hearing his voice again. It hit me like an unexpected left hook, knocking me off my center of balance. I stumbled, grabbing on to the rusted railing in an attempt to make it look if it were the height causing my unsteadiness.

"Preppy," I replied, clearing my throat when my voice came out scratchy and high pitched like a prepubescent boy.

There was no mistaking his sharp intake of breath.

"I heard you were dead. They had a funeral for you and everything you know," I said.

"I was never really a rule follower."

"You were never a law follower either but I never expected you to not listen to the laws of nature. You know. Life and death and all that. Most people don't come back from that."

"I'm not most people."

"That I know."

Preppy was sitting on the ledge on the far side, cloaked in the shadow of the tower. I could only make out the outline of his frame. There was a click of a lighter, the glowing flame hidden by his hand as he lit a cigarette and snapped the lighter shut.

"I heard the Causeway is a total tourist trap now," he said, responding to my earlier statement. "I heard everyone offs themselves there. It's too trendy. Every hipster from here to Miami is throwing themselves off that thing. I don't know if you know this about me, but I've never been much of a crowd follower."

"I think I might have heard that somewhere," I replied. I took a step toward him.

"No, Doc. Stay there," he demanded, the seriousness in his voice froze my foot mid-step. I lowered it back to the platform and was about to ask him why when he plead softly, "Please."

Not knowing where else to go I stepped over to the railing, stopping at the same spot where things could have turned out so much differently for me. I looked over the railing at the ground below.

"Long way down," Preppy pointed out.

"Would've been," I agreed, "but I never found out thanks to this guy who didn't want me haunting his precious tower." When I lifted my head I felt suddenly dizzy and had to close my eyes and take a deep breath, tilting my chin up to the bright moon and swaying on my feet.

"Steady there, Doc," Preppy said, his voice smooth, warming over me like a much needed blanket. "I didn't do shit. I followed the girl who stole from Mirna and by the time I got up here I saw a naked chick and wanted to touch her before she went splat. That's all that was." Preppy adjusted his position, his clothes rustling against the tower. "How is Mirna?"

"She passed. Six months ago," I said. "She held on for a really long time, longer than most hang on with her kind of dementia.

Funny thing was that when she died she hadn't been herself in so long, that in a way I was relieved."

"Sorry. For an old chick, she was a pretty fucking great one," Preppy said.

I thought about the way she forgave me after I stole from her. Gave me a place to stay. Gave me the benefit of the doubt when I didn't deserve it. "Yeah, yeah she was." I cleared my throat in an attempt to keep the tears at bay. "For never thinking I'd talk to you again; this is..."

"Fucking weird," Preppy inserted.

"Yeah," I agreed. "I was going to say amazing, but weird works too." I wrung my hands together and bit the inside of my lip.

"Amazing is just weird's older more mature sibling," Preppy pointed out.

I looked to the sky. "I had this list of things in my head. A list of things I would say to you if I ever had the chance again and now..."

"And now?" Preppy asked, like he wanted to know how that sentence ended.

"And right now I can't think of a single one of those things," I admitted.

"The weather," he said, suddenly.

"What?" I turned toward the shadowy corner, wishing I could see his face again.

"When people don't know what to say to one another they talk about the weather right? So.... shit's kind of hot tonight." A line of silver smoke from his exhale billowed into the air, grey smoke on top of black shadows.

I swallowed hard. "Yeah, it's hot," I said. "But if you want to talk news and current events I've heard there is a stalker out on the loose in Logan's Beach. He stands on back porches and glares into the windows of unassuming women."

"I think I heard that too. But it was just the window of one unassuming woman. And he's not a stalker."

"No?"

"More like a peeping tom."

I laughed and stepped toward him again, I could feel the argument on his lips, but before he could speak I sat down just outside of the dark space, only a foot or so away with my back against the tower next to a white tarp that was littered with buckets and brushes, smelling like fresh paint. "Why did you come to see me?"

"Why did you come to see me?" was his immediate reply. We were both quiet, probably because neither one of us could answer that question simply. "It's quiet here," he added.

"Yeah, it is."

"Since I've been home everything seems so fucking loud," he lamented.

"Preppy, what happened to y…"

He cut me off before I could finish. "No, Doc. Not now. Not today. Probably not fucking ever." I looked over and saw the burning red glow of the cherry burn brighter as he inhaled, wishing it was just a bit brighter so I could catch a glimpse of the lips attached to end of that cigarette.

He must have been looking at me too. "I like your glasses," he said.

"Thanks," I said, pushing them up on my nose. "My vision had been a little blurry for years. I always thought it was because of the heroin, or maybe that's just why I didn't care. It wasn't until after I got clean and it didn't get any better that I went and got my eyes checked. I was still in shock when they told me it wasn't the heroin after all. It was just me." I laughed nervously. "Guess you're probably surprised I managed to stay clean after all this time."

"No, I always knew you'd kick that shit," Preppy said, the confidence in his voice taking me by surprise. He took a deep breath. "Doc, I have to say this. Four years ago…"

"Preppy, no. You don't have to," I interrupted. "You're not obligated to say anything about what happened back then. It was so long ago. It's all been long forgotten," I lied.

"Fours years ago," he started again, with more determination. "I was a complete shit to you. Thought about it a lot since then. Thought I could just push you away instead of dealing with how mixed up I was feeling. I just wanted to send it all to the back of my brain and keep it there." He laughed like he couldn't believe his own words. "For years I thought I was such a badass because you leaving didn't affect me like it ought to of. Truth is that it did. A fucking lot. I just didn't let it show, and for some stupid reason in my mind I thought that it was the same as not affecting me. It only took being mostly alone in the dark for months on end to realize how fucking ridiculous that really was."

What the fuck happened to you, Preppy?

"I thought that way for a long time too," I admitted. "And that's one of the reasons I'm here. In town. For closure. I've made so many mistakes. So freaking many."

"Did you find it?" Preppy asked. "Your closure?

I looked over to the dark corner and felt his eyes on me when I whispered, "Not even close." I pressed my teeth against my lower lip. I sighed and let my head fall back against the water tower.

"Why not?" Preppy asked.

I looked up at the perfect cloudless night sky and the thousands of twinkling stars overhead. I closed my eyes tightly. "Because I found you instead."

A pair of squawking black birds chose that moment to practically fall from the night sky, tangled up with one another. My eyes shot open to the scene playing out in front of us. The birds would separate briefly, only to fly another few feet before colliding together again, talons extended, beaks pecking away at the other. The occasional feather floated down onto the platform. The pair traded blow for blow as they rose and fell in the air like a carnival ride. "You think they're fighting or fucking?" I asked, not realizing I'd spoken the words out loud until it was too late.

The mood between us turned more serious. Even the crickets must have realized the shift in energy because it was as if they'd sensed it and stopped chirping so they could listen in. "I think you and I both know you can be doing both at the same time." His words took me right back to when Bear became a tool in our battle of 'who could make each other feel worse'.

If there was a winner, it sure as shit hadn't been me.

"Who knew that sex could be the ultimate weapon of mass destruction?" I asked, followed by a nervous laugh. I reached for the ends of the sleeves I wasn't wearing so I could pull them down over my hands. I could feel his eyes on me, watching my every move. I shifted left and right, already feeling the indentations of the diamond plated metal platform taking shape on my butt cheeks. "So… more weather then?" I asked, needing to break the tension that was winding tighter and tighter in the space between us before it broke.

"More anything else," Preppy replied, sounding both relieved and saddened.

"Learn anything new since you've been…" I hesitated, not knowing what word to use. "Back?"

"Well," Preppy started. "King and his girl got a bunch of kids now. They rebuilt the garage because there was some sort of catastrophic event that they won't tell me about. But then again they aren't really telling me shit these days. Bear is hiding from me for some reason. My room is now bubblegum pink and is being occupied by a six year old who likes to come in my room and stare at me while I sleep." He paused. "And Grace died."

"I'm so sorry," I said, reaching my hand out to comfort him only to be met with the cold metal of the tower when he skidded back out of reach. I retracted my hand and pulled my knees into my chest.

"Forget the weather. Maybe tell me something funny. Tell me a joke, Doc," his voice was fading as if he were growing tired. "I haven't heard one of those in a long while."

I sat for a second, breathing in the smell of cigarette smoke and his soap, thinking I was in some sort of dream that was about to end. All of my dreams about Preppy ended abruptly so if it was a dream, time wasn't on my side. "Knock knock," I started.

"Who's there?"

I hesitated and almost changing my mind about what I was going to say next, but I needed to rescue the words dangling from my lips before I woke up from this weird dream and it was too late.

"Who's there, Doc?" Preppy asked in a whisper.

I took a deep breath. "Me."

"Me who?" He asked, playing along.

"Apparently…your wife."

Silence.

I cleared my throat. "Those papers I left for you?" I started, "The documents you wanted to use to get guardianship of King's daughter? Those were just meant for show for the lawyers and the judge, but very recently, like VERY recently, I learned that you filed the marriage license. So in the eyes of the county clerk's office…well, in the eyes of the State of Florida as a whole…"

"We're married," Preppy finished, not sounding the least bit surprised.

"Yeah," I replied. "We're married."

"Guess I just got confused," he said, shifting his position although I couldn't see exactly how I heard the scraping of metal against the platform which I assumed must have been a button on his pants. "All that shit with Max was over my head. Probably thought I was supposed to file them." He explained in a manner that had me thinking there was more to what he was saying that he wasn't letting on.

He loves you, you fucking idiot. He sent you that letter. He told you he loved you. He filed them because HE LOVES YOU.

"Why are you back, Doc? Here? In Logan's Beach?"

"When I went home my dad sent me to rehab. The best in New York. My dad's business had always done alright so I didn't question him when I asked where the money was coming from to pay for it and he lied to me and told me his insurance was paying for it." I took a deep breath and remembered the reassuring look on his face when he tried to convince me it would all be okay.

"But it wasn't."

"No, it wasn't insurance. There was no insurance. It was all him. He took out all these loans. First to send me to rehab and then back to school," I cringed because I hated the fact that my father sacrificed so much because of all my mistakes. "Long story short, his business is failing. Or, according to the past due notices and demands for payment I've found, it's already failed."

"And?"

"And he's losing his house," I replied. "Because of me."

"That's not your fault," Preppy said, sounding a lot like Brandon.

"I know," I agreed, although it was a lie. "But that doesn't mean that I'm not going to try and do my damnedest to help him."

"You're selling the house?" Preppy guessed.

"Yeah, I'm selling the house. How did you know?"

"Either I could see where your story was going… or maybe it was that big ass for sale sign in Mirna's front yard might have tipped me off," he said. "I mean; the stalker might have seen it when he stalked by."

"I see," I said, my lips turning up into a smile.

"You know those letters I told you I wrote in case of my untimely death?" Preppy asked.

"Yeah?" I froze.

"Well I kept them up and I left instructions for Doe…I mean Ray, King's girl, to send them out for me after…" I heard him shift and he stretched out his legs, his black boots were now visible in the light.

"Ray came to see me today. I like her," I admitted.

"She did?" Preppy asked.

"Yeah, just wanted to say hi," I said, "So what happened, with the letters?"

"Well…I wrote you one," Preppy said, lighting another

cigarette. "But I guess I only wrote DRE on the outside of the envelope," he chuckled. "No address."

"Why is that funny?" I asked.

"It's funny because Doe didn't want to open it and invade my privacy. When she cleaned out my music collection, like my old CD's and shit, she noticed I had a lot of NWA stuff and old school Dre and Snoop."

"Okay?" I asked, confused as to where he was going and how on earth west coast rappers played a part in the story.

"She told me she held my letter up to the light to see if it had an address inside, but all she could make out was the first line, which said Doc."

Suddenly, I understood where he was going. "No, she didn't," I exclaimed with a squeal, covering my mouth with my hand.

"Oh yes she did. She sent my letter to Dr. Dre, the rapper, via the Dr. Dre fan club."

"Holy shit!" I bent over, holding my stomach so the laughter wouldn't split me in two.

"No, Doc, wait. That's not the holy shit part. The holy shit part…is what they sent back."

"Do I want to know?" I asked, leaning in toward him.

"They send back an autographed headshot of Dr. Dre and…"

"And?" I egged him on, eager to hear the rest.

"And…a restraining order," he finished.

We both burst out into a fit of laughter. After calming down I remembered that when I received the letter from Preppy it was delivered by a courier service out of L.A. I thought it was odd at the time, but had more pressing matters at hand. Like a letter from PREPPY. I could recite every word from that letter. I could describe how he slants his letters to the left and how his y's dip so low below the line they run into the sentence below. So of course I remembered that my address WAS on the inside. Whoever must have opened it at the fan club must have had it forwarded it to me.

He thinks I never received it.

"What did the letter say?" I asked tentatively after our laughter had died down. I immediately regretted it. It wasn't like he was really going to tell me.

I was right.

Preppy paused. "Nothing important. You know. This and that. Probably just some stuff about the weather."

After a comfortable beat of silence Preppy was the one who spoke first, "Did you see what they did to this thing?" he asked, followed by a rap of his knuckles against the side of the metal tower.

"What do you mean?" I asked.

"The paint? I guess they finally splurged on something that was able to cover the big black dick I spray painted way back when. They killed my fucking masterpiece." He said, and with the new shift in topic I immediately felt lighter. "Bastards."

"The shame," I said, feigning shock. "Although they only covered it in the last week or two, because I saw it from the plane when I landed."

"You saw it from the plane?" He asked with amazement in his voice. "And they had to go and cover it up. It was like a fucking landmark. Greatest thing to happen to this town since the tourists realized our little slum had a white sandy beach attached to it." He laughed softly. "It was always good for a chuckle or two when I could see the faint outline of it on the postcards they sell at those little tourist trap shops."

"Well," I smacked my hands against my knees and stood up. I rummaged through the paint buckets, feeling Preppy's eyes on me as I bent over to survey the tools at hand. "We'll just need to fix that then won't we?" When I turned back around I was holding a can of black spray paint, presumably what they'd used to darken the LOGAN'S BEACH lettering. "So what do you say?" I shook the can and it made that clacking sound that only spray paint cans made. "Shall we?"

"Another time, Doc. Come sit back down," Preppy yawned and I reluctantly set down the paint and did as he asked, taking a seat in my spot just outside his shadowland.

"Did I do that?" he suddenly asked. Realizing I couldn't see him he added, "Your neck, that was me wasn't it."

I shook my head. "No. I mean yes, you freaked out and went for my throat, but that just left some red marks. That was weeks ago. Those are all gone." I covered the cut on my neck with my hand. "But this was from a fight with a weed-whacker. In case you didn't already know…I didn't win."

"Fuck," he groaned, sounding like he was in pain. He reared up on his feet in a crouched position, like he was either afraid to step into the light, or debating on staying or leaving.

"You don't have to go," I said, my voice a whisper.

A few seconds passed. A horn honked in the distance. "Will you lay with me?" he asked, sounding tired. "Just for a while? I haven't been sleeping for shit."

"Here?" I asked.

"Here. Turn around. On your side."

I did as he asked and laid down on the cold platform onto my side facing away from him. He slowly moved up behind me, and then I felt him. The second his skin connected to mine it was like changing a lightbulb that had been burnt out for a long time. Bright and electric and warm was what I felt as he draped his arm over mine. His thumb brushed over my hand and I shivered. He exhaled in a deep sigh as if he could feel the new light between us. "We're still the same you know," he whispered.

I turned my head to ask him what he meant, but he stopped me with his hand, gently turning my face away from him. "Don't look."

"You don't have to hide from me, Preppy. I've already seen you."

"I know," he replied, holding me tighter, and just like that I felt it. The light grew to a full electrical storm. There was a charge in the air, energy all around us. He laced his fingers with mine and I swear my heart stopped beating. "I know," he repeated. He exhaled, his breath skating across the back of my neck, his lips against my skin. "But maybe I'm the one hiding from me."

It was the last thing Preppy said before his breathing evened out. With Preppy wrapped around me I drifted off shortly after.

When I woke up the next day the sun was high in the sky, it's hot rays burning holes in my retinas.

I was alone.

For a brief moment I thought it was all a dream until my eyes adjusted to the harsh light and landed on the newly spray-painted big black cock scrawled on the side of the tower.

CHAPTER SEVEN

PREPPY

I WAS BEYOND RESTLESS.

I'd decided that the reason I couldn't sleep was because the mattress was too soft. I slid down to the floor, but I couldn't turn off my mind. I only fell asleep for a short time on the tower with Dre, but it was the deepest sleep I'd gotten besides being in a fucking coma. When I woke up I spent a long time smelling her hair like the creep I was before deciding that the big black cock needed to make a comeback.

I was happy for her. For getting clean. For going to school. For wanting to help out her dad. No, I wasn't happy, that wasn't the right word.

I was PROUD.

But pride couldn't stop the selfish thought that nagged at the back of my brain that missed when Dre was a junkie and a mess so that I could somehow come to her rescue again. There were two problems with that thought.

One, she didn't need to be saved.

Two, I was in no fucking shape to be anyone's knight.

Fuck, she was so beautiful.

Dre didn't need a stitch of makeup. Her long lashes and

plump pink lips made her a flawless natural beauty. The new glasses were like a nerdy bonus that brought more attention to her big dark eyes.

I wondered if she still wore the fifties style clothes, the heels, and my fucking favorite…the red lips.

I rolled onto my back and slid my hand down into my pants as I thought about those lips. I remembered what they felt like against mine. I regret never having had the chance to see them wrapped around my dick. I remember what her pussy tasted like more than I remembered what coffee tasted like. The noises she made when she was about to come assaulted my memory. That memory gave way to our first time. The way she fought back against me but loved every fucking second of it when I fucked her by the train tracks. It was then I realized she was almost as sick as I was. That moment of my life was better than any porn reel and over the years it had been my number one mental image to jerk off to. Yet after a few minutes my dick was still flaccid.

Not a twinge. Not a fucking spark.

I tugged on my balls and rubbed the sensitive strip of skin underneath them. I then brought my hand to my shaft and ran my palm over it, willing it back to life. I took a deep breath and thought about the way Dre's tits bounced in my hand when I fucked her from behind. The way she moaned and tensed her thigh muscles when she was about to come.

Not a motherfucking thing.

I might have been alive, but my cock was still fucking dead.

I released my useless dick and let my head fall back against the carpet releasing a growl of frustration. It may not have gotten hard but I needed to come, to release. It was the only way I knew how to rid myself of the lingering bullshit in my brain and try to clear some space for all the other shit floating around up there.

You're still healing, asshole. Get a fucking grip. I told myself.

When the sun was high in the sky and I could feel the heat of its rays through the closed window I finally gave up on both sleep, and a hard cock.

I made my way out into the living room.

The second I took that last step down I was assaulted by light. I shielded my eyes with my forearms from the onslaught coming through the front window. Using my palm to fight against the blinding rays, I shuffled over to the wall and reached out for the metal string so I could close the blinds, but it wasn't there. Peeking through the slits in my eyes I realized the long off white plastic blinds that used to clank together when the air conditioning kicked on were no longer there. In their place was a more modern wooden shutter. I found the crank and turned it, sighing in relief when I again found myself in the comforts of the dark. I blinked rapidly to get rid of the stars still dancing behind my eyes.

I thought I was alone until I spun around to find Doe looking up at me from the kitchen. She gasped, covering her hand with her mouth as she looked me up and down, taking in my shaved head and hair free face for the first time. When she realized she was staring she averted her gaze down to the messenger bag she was organizing on the counter and cleared her throat. "Um... do the clothes I brought you not fit?" She zipped up the bag and lifted her eyes to me, doing a better job of hiding her shock at my appearance, only her dilating pupils gave her true feelings away.

"I'm good," I said, glancing down at my t-shirt and sweats. "I don't need much. When did you guys remodel?" I asked taking in the new wood floors and fresh paint. Even the cabinets were the same but had been sanded and painted a bright white. "Looks like adults live here now," I said.

"Which is funny because it's overrun by kids," Doe said with a smile. She pushed up the strap of her tank top that kept falling off her shoulder.

"Preppy, if you don't like the color of the shirt or bow ties I can get you different colors, or you can come with me to pick out your own. There's this new store called GENTS across the causeway with an entire wall of bowties, but it's only open during the season so we'll have to wait to go there when it's open again in November. We might have to fight off some tourists for best pick of the new stuff they put out, but it could be fun."

I shrugged. "Jeans would be good."

"Remember when you bought me that dress for our 'date?'" she asked, using air quotes when she said the word 'date.' "It fit perfectly and you didn't even know my size. Shit, I didn't even know my size. The skirt I was wearing was from the hooker ready section of goodwill and whatever hooker wore it before me had an ass that went on for days." Doe lamented with a laugh. "That was a long time ago," she added.

"To me that was yesterday," I said.

The smile slowly fell from her face and she changed the subject. "Did you make a list of things you needed?" I loved that girl like a sister but the way she looked at me like I was a sad puppy dog with a broken leg was starting to piss me off.

"It's on the counter." I opened the refrigerator and grabbed a beer.

"What the fuck is this?" Doe asked, waving the list around in the air.

"You asked me to make you a list of the shit I wanted."

"I meant like groceries," Doe jutted out a hip.

"What do you think that is?" I popped open the beer on the corner of the counter and cringed, holding a hand over my right ear until the echoing faded. I cracked my jaw like I was popping my ears on an airplane but I knew that a little jaw popping wouldn't be enough to cure me of my aversions to sound and light.

I was like a reverse Helen Keller.

I plopped on the couch and picked up the remote, clicking through channels.

Doe came to stand in front of me, blocking my view of the screen as she read back my list. "Blow, weed, the last three seasons of American Ninja Warrior, non-shitty beer, Johnny Walker, Jose Cuervo..." she stopped and crumpled the paper. "This isn't a fucking shopping list, Preppy, it's a list of felonies." She threw the wad of paper at me and it bounced off my face, rolling onto the floor. "Give that kind of shit to King or Bear, in the meantime, if you need clothes, or food, or things like deodorant and toothpaste, then I'm your gal."

"Why are you so pissed off at me?" I asked, taking my eyes from the TV to give her a questioning look.

"Because...I don't fucking know!" She snapped, grabbing her bag from the counter and swung open the front door.

"Where are you going?"

"The kids are at school and the baby is with King in his studio so I'm going to the food store to get stuff for dinner, and then I'm going to Grace's grave to lay fresh flowers and then pick up the kids and then tonight I have an appointment to tattoo an entire butt cheek with the face of a tiger. "You can come with me, you know. To Grace's grave?"

"Nah, I'm good here," I said, taking a swig of my beer and turning back around to the TV. "Wait, when did you start tattooing?" I called out but she was already gone.

The screen slammed shut and if the sound of her stomping down the steps indicated how she felt about my refusal to take her up on her offer to go to the cemetery, then Doe was most defiantly pissed the fuck off. It took a solid minute of covering my ears and rocking back and forth for those sounds to stop bouncing around in my head.

I rubbed my eyes. "Chicks," I muttered, sitting back against the cushions.

"She kind of has a point there," someone said. I turned my head to the hallway as a girl with long pinkish hair and a very big baby belly stepped out from the back door into the living room. She leaned against the wall next to the TV. "You haven't gone to the cemetery since they told you about Grace. You should go with her sometime."

"You mean since I *found out* about Grace," I corrected her, unable to hide the bitterness from my voice. "No point. Just a box in the ground surrounded by other buried boxes in the ground. Never did make much sense to me to visit people who can't talk back."

"Did you know that Ray visits your grave while she's there too? Brings you flowers and everything. Even since you've come back. She's still been doing it. I don't know if it's out of habit or…"

"Or why?" I asked. "What exactly are you getting at oh wise pink one?"

"Or maybe she's still visiting your grave because she feels like you haven't really come back yet."

It was my turn to roll my eyes. "That's ridiculous, I'm right fucking here…wait, I have a grave?" I again lifted my feet onto the table and expected her to slide hers off to make room. No such luck. Oh she lifted her feet alright, but the second my heels came in contact with the table she rested them across my shins and sighed deeply. "That's creepy as fuck…and kind of fucking cool."

"Don't you want to know who I am?" she asked.

"I was getting to that," I lied, staring daggers at her offending feet resting across my legs. The girl gave me an eerie sense of deja-vu and although I was positive I didn't know this her, I kind of felt like I knew about her.

"I'm Thia, Bear's fiancé," she offered. "But you can call me Ti if you want." She patted her stomach and smiled. "This here is Trey. Well, Trey if it's a boy, or Jackie Marie if it's a girl."

"Bear?" I asked, the mention of his name grating against my nerves. The fucker still hadn't shown his face. "I don't know a Bear. I mean, the name sounds vaguely familiar but I can't quite picture him. Sounds ugly as fuck though."

It would sound more familiar if he showed his fucking face and stopped avoiding me.

Thia rolled her eyes. "He's giving you time, asshole. Take it as a gift because trust me, you fucking need it."

"Time for what?" I asked, pushing her legs off of mine and sitting up so I could lean in and better glare at the stranger in front of me. "And what the fuck is that supposed to mean?"

"You'll find out."

"Thanks pink haired Dali-lama, I feel much better about one of my best friends ignoring me now that you've explained everything. Shit's all fucking roses again." I chugged down the rest of my beer and set it harshly down on the table, the bottom of the bottle made a loud SMACK against the glass.

"Why don't you focus on what's important, Preppy?"

"And what exactly is that?"

"The fact that Ray is at the cemetery right now putting flowers on your fucking head stone when you're alive and right here, sitting in her fucking living room."

"MY living room," I corrected.

"See? That's exactly what I mean. You're not focusing on what's important." Thia said, standing up slowly in a series of small motions a lot like a semi truck making an eight point u-turn on a narrow road. "Also, she didn't want to tell you but she's been going to see Dre. They've become pretty good friends."

"Wait, what?" I asked, but she too was already across the house. What was with people telling me part of a fact before taking off?

"Chicks," I muttered again when I thought she'd gone back out the same door she'd entered.

"I heard that!" Thia said from behind me. I jumped and dropped my empty bottle onto the floor.

"You were supposed to!" I said back, picking the bottle off the floor and setting it back on the coffee table. I rounded the couch and grabbed a fresh beer from the fridge, feeling Thia's gaze on me the entire time. When I sat back on the couch I felt the back of my neck where I could have sworn her stare was burning a hole in my skin. "You sure know how to make an impression," I said.

"Well, now at least you'll remember me," she said, this time making her way to the back door and opening it.

"Pregnant girl with pink hair, no filter, and boundary issues. Don't think I'll have any trouble remembering who you are," I said, raising my beer to her in a mock cheers before taking a long pull from the bottle.

She paused and smiled brightly. "Well, if you do find yourself a little sluggish on the details and you can't quite remember who I am there is one tiny thing about me that might be able to jog your memory in a pinch."

"Oh yeah?" I asked, "Lay it on me Thia. What is it that will make you so memorable?"

She winked. "You can just remember me as that chick who killed Chop."

CHAPTER EIGHT

PREPPY

I WAS BEGINNING TO think the excuses that everyone was giving me about Bear's absence was utter bullshit until he finally showed up, standing in the doorway on the front porch, his massive frame taking up every inch of available space. He peered into the living room. "Prep?" he asked, taking a tentative step toward me.

"About fucking time, bitch. Get your big ass over here. You can't catch what I have although if you could I wouldn't put it past you to already have it." I paused as he entered the room because pure panic rose in my blood. The deep blue eyes, the freckles, the size, the posture, everything about him screamed RUN to me.

I straightened my spine and set my feet into the carpet, pushing back against the cushions of the couch until I tipped it over on it's side. I stumbled over it, not able to take my eyes off the figure moving toward me. The one that haunted me. "No!" I cried as I shuffled against the wall to find the door.

He'd come for me. I needed to escape but it was too late. Before I could reach the door he was on me, his hands on my arms holding me in place. I closed my eyes tightly and braced myself for the blow, for the pain, because that's what always came next.

The pain.

Only it never came.

"Preppy! It's me, it's Bear. I'm not my old man. I wouldn't fucking hurt you like that cock sucker did. Do you hear me? I WOULD NEVER. FUCKING. HURT YOU!" he screamed.

Something familiar in his voice triggered me to slowly come back to reality and open my eyes. Much to my relief it wasn't Chop standing there with concern written all over his face. "You would never hurt me," I repeated slowly. Bear nodded, his breath ragged. He loosened his grip on my shoulders.

"Never," he said.

I nodded slowly and he released me, taking a step back. I leaned over to compose myself, shaking off the adrenaline coursing through my veins. "Never."

"Never."

The fog cleared and I stood up straight, looking over my old friend, "Even if I fucked your girlfriend?"

"Never. I mean, I'd fucking kill you, but I wouldn't hurt you. I'd make it real quick though. You know, 'cause we're brothers and all."

"Awe. You're such a romantic, Care Bear," I was still trying to catch my breath.

"And you're such an asshole, Prep," Bear said, shoving his thumbs through the belt loops of his black jeans.

"Well at least now I know why you didn't come sooner," I admitted. "And I was motherfucking you to everyone who'd listen."

"I know. I heard." Bear smiled. "Now come here you alive,

motherfucker." He pulled me in for one of the only hugs Bear has ever voluntarily given me and the need to make fun of him lingered just under the need to be reunited with the other half of the duo that made of my best friends.

There we stood, in the middle of the living room, hugging it out, each trying to hold back our tears until our need to cry outweighed our need to be the manly fucking men we were and we were no longer able to hold in the tears.

"I'm not fucking crying," Bear sobbed.

"Me neither, you fucking pussy," I sobbed back as my old friend held me tighter and we hugged and punched each other hard on the backs until I was sure we were going to give each other bruises, and if it went on much longer, probably some broken ribs. When he finally let go of me we quickly wiped our eyes and noses on our t-shirts, because real men don't fucking cry, and that's when I noticed the new tattoo on the back of Bear's neck.

"Bear?" I asked, as he pulled a pack of smokes out from his cut. "What is that?" I sang, pointing to the very reason why I'd be able to make fun of Bear for the rest of his fucking life. "Is that what I think it is?" I stepped behind him to try and get a better look.

Realizing what I was gaping at he quickly covered the back of his neck with his hand and stepped back against the wall. "That ain't nothing."

"No, Bear," I said, slowly approaching him. "That's a tattoo that says PREP. It's…EVERYTHING…"

Bear dropped his hand and rolled his eyes. He smiled as he retrieved his lighter. "Fine, motherfucker. I thought your ass was dead so I got a tattoo of your name on the back of my neck. I realize that you've probably thought of a thousand dumb shit things to say about it already, but can we just skip that part for now? There will be plenty of time for that later. Besides, I'm going to get it covered up with like a dragon or a tattoo of Chuck Norris or something really fucking manly."

I looked him in the eye and held up my index finger. "You get one pass. Just this ONE. And it's TEMPORARY."

"You're too fucking kind. Now here," Bear said, reaching down into a saddle bag that was right outside the door. "This is for you," he tossed me an extra deep shirt box.

"What the fuck is this?" I asked, following him outside onto the front porch.

"Consider it a Preppy starter kit," Bear said.

I set it down on the back of the railing and opened it up to find several shirts, suspenders, and bow tie sets. I closed the lid and set it aside. "Thanks, man."

"When you're ready," Bear said, pointing to the box. "Just for when you're ready." For all the shit I gave him Bear always had an uncanny way of understanding me and knowing when not to push.

I nodded.

"Now look under the clothes," he said the cigarette dangling from his bottom lip.

I cast him a 'what the fuck are you up to' look and opened the box back up. I felt around under the clothes at the bottom of the box. I pulled out a carton of cigarettes, a plastic bag with several already rolled joints, and a box of magnum sized condoms.

"Again, for when you're ready," Bear said, this time with a sly smile. He handed me two more boxes, that had been sitting next to his saddle bag on the deck, the smaller one on top contained smart phone and the larger one on the bottom a laptop. The boxes looked new, but the plastic wrapping had been removed.

"Thanks man." I fished out a joint from the baggie and rolling it under my nose, inhaling deeply. "God I missed that smell."

"Well, the weed and smokes are from me and King. Ti and Ray picked out the clothes. Ti even went as far as taking the laptop to the geek guy at the tech store and had him bookmark all sorts of weird porn sites for you. I looked at some of them, made my skin crawl so I think you'll dig it."

Fuck, I was kind of a dick to her…

"I met your girl the other day, she seems…interesting," I said. Bear smiled. "She told me she was the one who pulled the trigger on…" I couldn't bring myself to say his name. "That true?"

Bear nodded. "Yeah, she saved my fucking life, too. I'll tell you this, you don't know what love really is until you see your girl wipe your evil old man from the face of the fucking earth for you."

"Fuck, I think I kind of love her too." Bear was looking off into the distance like he was recalling a memory. "Think she'd be down for a pity fuck?" I asked, holding up the box of condoms.

"I'm going to pretend you didn't fucking say that," Bear said, his nostrils flared. He knocked the box from my hands.

"You're such a brute," I said, placing the joint between my lips and held my hand out for Bear's lighter.

Bear shook his head. "No fucking way, man. You're gonna have to go to the garage and hide in a fucking corner like the rest of us have to. Dead or not, Ray will toss you off the fucking balcony if you smoke weed by the house."

"Since fucking when?"

"Since we got Sammy, Max, and Nicole running around here

and are about to add to the litter with my kid. No smoking that shit until the kids are either asleep or at school, and even then it's still only in the fucking garage."

"Sammy?"

"You don't know the kids' names?"

I leaned over the railing, grateful that the sun was setting because it meant the pressure behind my eyes would ease up once it was tucked into the horizon for the night. "I mean, Doe told gave me the cliffs notes about the kids and I've heard them yelling at them. I knew the girl was Max and the boy was Doe's…I mean, Ray's, kid, but I never really thought about his name before."

"Yeah, turns out she named her kid Samuel years before she met you, how ironic is that? Now we got two of you running around. He's a good kid. Funny as shit too. One week he's trying to copy me by wearing his own little cut and wanting to ride a bike and the next week he's got belts around his arms 'cause he wants to be like King. Get to know him. And the girls." Bear turned sideways to face me, leaning his elbow against the rail. He pointed his smoke at me as he spoke. "Those kids are the best things that have happened to this place in a long fucking time."

I absentmindedly went to light the joint again and Bear raised his eyebrows. I pulled it from my lips. "I can't smoke a fucking joint in my own house? How do you people live like this?" I asked, appalled.

It's not your house anymore.

He slapped me on the back. "One fucking breath at a time, brother."

"I don't think I was just gone for a while," I said, tossing the joint back into the bag. "I think I fucking upset the space time continuum. You've got a girl, and I can't freely engage in my love of illegal narcotics. What the fuck?" I realized I sounded like whiny kid, well, a whiny kid who wants to smoke a joint on his porch, but I was unable to stop the very real confusion that I was feeling.

A part of me, a VERY selfish part of me, always hoped that while I was gone the world was somehow on pause. But it wasn't. The world moved on.

They all moved on.

"This bullshit, Prep, is called being an adult," Bear said, slapping me on the back. "Fucking sucks, don't it?" He laughed but his expression told me he thought it anything BUT fucking sucked.

"I can't believe you've got a girl," I said. "If I had to bet between you settling down and the zombie apocalypse, my money would've been on the zombies. So much has happened while I was…gone."

Bear flashed me a sad smile. The kind of smile everyone was giving me since I'd woken up. The kind of smile that was making me both furious and sick to my fucking stomach. "So does your girl know you're in love with me?" I asked, looking at his neck again before tucking the joint behind my ear.

"Prep," Bear warned. "Later."

"Buzzkill," I muttered.

"And yeah I got a girl. Good one too. Knocked her up and everything," Bear said proudly. He lit his cigarette and tossed me his lighter.

"Wow, you waited until I was gone to become the grand marshall of white trash?" I tapped the bottom the fresh pack against my hand a few times before pulling one out and lighting my own. The first inhale of smoke filling my lungs felt fucking

GLORIOUS and gave me an instant high I hadn't had from a cigarette since I was a kid, toking on my first smoke behind the portables at school.

"Nah, cause I put a ring on her finger, too."

"There goes the parade I was gonna throw you."

"Prep, Ti and I have been staying in the garage apartment while the club is undergoing a little bit of a makeover," Bear said.

"What kind of makeover? Like a Renovation?"

"It's a little more *involved*."

I shrugged and took another drag. "Well, that place was always a shit hole. It could use some paint or getting rid of the swamp you guys call a pool in the middle of that damn thing. What did you start with?"

"Hazmat suits and blood removal."

"Good call."

"I thought so," Bear leaned forward on the railing, looking out onto the ground below. "But since Grace…"

"Yeah…" I interrupted, letting him know there was no need to finish his sentence in order to site the grim obvious.

"Ti and I are gonna move over to Grace's house real soon. I'm thinking 'bout eventually buying some property on the other side of the bay and building something over there. Word is old man Jenson's looking to sell, but I figured for now we'll post up over at Grace's house so we have some room after the baby's born."

"Grace's house?" I asked. "You bought Grace's house?"

Bear smirked. "Nope. Didn't buy it." He glanced over at me. "They didn't tell you did they?"

I shook my head. "What, motherfucker? Tell me!" I demanded, stubbing out my cigarette on the bottom of my shoe.

Bear's smile grew brighter. *Shit, when did he get so many fucking teeth?* "Prep, as it turns out, Grace was my Grandma."

"Holy fucking shit." The first thought that hit me was pure fucking joy. "Man, I'm jealous as fuck, but that just might be the greatest thing I've ever seen or heard. Like ever."

"Yeah, just might be," Bear agreed.

"Well," I pointed at his neck. "Maybe next to that fucking tattoo.

CHAPTER NINE

DRE

"I WISH YOU WEREN'T leaving tomorrow," I said to Brandon as we waited for the realtor to arrive. The house still needed some work. I hadn't yet started on either the gutters or the painting but Brandon suggested we talk to a professional to see what they thought about listing price and sale time. Especially since I hadn't gotten so much as a single call from my FOR SALE BY OWNER ads.

"I wish I could stay longer, too. But Ralph called this morning and it seems that the entire world is going to crumble if I don't return by the weekend. At least, you know Ralph, that's how he makes it sound. It's only been a few weeks but alas, I am missed."

Just then a newer model Honda pulled up and a tall man in his early to mid thirties stepped out. He had a lean build and wore jeans with a white button down and a blue blazer. His hair was slicked back and he wore thick black framed glasses that reminded me of my own. His boots were bright red and pointed at the toe.

"Hi, you must be...Andrea, is it?" he asked with a big smile, shaking my hand. "I'm Easton Feather, but you just you can just call me East because that's what all my friends call me and I can tell from the second that we spoke on the phone that we are going to be great friends."

I smiled at his enthusiasm. "Yes, I'm Andrea, but you can just call me Dre. This is my friend Brandon," I said, and the two men shook hands.

"Do I know you? You look familiar?" East said to me, pulling his glasses down the bridge of his nose.

"I don't think so, but I used to come here every summer so you might have seen me around."

East snapped his fingers. "That must be it. It's a small town and feels even smaller when you overhear how some of the women gossip around here." East fanned himself with his clipboard and looked up at the house over my shoulder.

"So Dre," East started, as I told you on the phone that I recommend that we tour the property first so I can see what we're working with and then I'll pull up some comparable homes that have sold in the area recently so we can get a better idea of price. Then I'll go over my listing plan with you and let you know what I'm going to be doing in terms of marketing like hosting an open house, posting on the latest real estate apps, and so on." He looked up at the house and made a few scribbles on his clipboard. "Sound good? Shall we?" he asked, ascending the porch steps and letting himself in the front door without waiting for an answer.

"I guess we shall," Brandon said with a laugh as we followed East into the house.

Over the next two hours East did exactly what he'd promised and made a full evaluation of the house as well as a plan to sell and market with a full list of comps. After taking pictures for the listing he shook our hands and said good-bye, promising to email me the link to the listing in the morning before it went live.

"He's an…odd one," Brandon whispered without moving his lips as we waved back to East who had just pulled out of the driveway and taken off down the road.

"I like him," I said. "He's nice. And honestly as long as he can do what he says he can with the house he can be as different as he wants to be."

"True story," Brandon said, holding open the front door for me while I passed through under his arm. "Wanna help me pack?"

"But you aren't leaving until tomorrow," I started to whine. But then I saw something in the corner of my eye, something in the back yard. When I went to the window and spied out the back I could have sworn what I saw hoping over the fence was a little kid. He disappeared as quickly as he'd appeared.

"What?" Brandon asked, standing beside me at the window. "What did you see?"

"I think there was a kid in the backyard," I said, opening the back sliding door and shuffling over to the back gate with Brandon on my heels.

"A kid? Like small and scraggly looking?"

"Yeah? I thought you said you didn't see anything."

"I didn't. Not right now, anyway. But the other day I was pulling out when I saw him standing behind me in the rearview mirror. By the time I turned around he was running away. Must just be a kid from around here, curious as to who his new neighbor lady is."

"Yeah, must be…" I said walking back to the house with Brandon. My phone buzzed.

"Hello?"

"So we're having a party tonight," Ray practically shouted in my ear. "Come to the house around nine. One of the GG's is watching the kids at her house so we're going to have a big bonfire. Lot's of booze. Be here or I'm coming to get you myself!" Ray didn't give me a chance to answer. The line went dead.

"Party?" Brandon questioned. "I mean; I could go for a party." He paused. "Or would it be too weird for you to be there?"

The sound of a branch snapping caught my attention and I turned back to the woods. There was a slight rustling of the brush. I waited and listened.

Nothing.

"Dre, did you hear me?" Brandon asked. "Would it be too strange for you to be there? You know, since HE is going to be there."

"Stranger things have happened," I said, still looking out into the woods.

"Huh? No offense, but…what the fuck are you talking about?" he asked. "I'm talking about a party and you're looking out into space like you just saw the ghost of Christmas future or some crap."

"Party. Me. You. Got ya. I'm in," I said, heading back into the house with an eerie sense of dread looming over me. I didn't know if it was because of the party and the thought of seeing him again, or because when all the hairs on my arm stood on end I couldn't shake a certain feeling.

A feeling like I was being watched.

CHAPTER TEN

PREPPY

"HEY! GET YOUR ass up and come to the garage. We have something for you," King boomed from the bottom of the porch. I sat on the front steps of fucking around with my new laptop. "What the fuck are you doing?"

"Looking up nude pics of your mom."

"Turn off the porn and come with me," he demanded.

"I'm not even looking at porn. Just checking to see what the fuck's been going on in the world since I dropped off the face of it," I admitted.

"Anything interesting?" King asked, putting a cigarette between his lips but not lighting it.

"Well, it seems I missed the election," I said.

"For what?" King asked.

"President."

"Of what?"

"Of the United States."

"Of what?" King asked, again.

I glanced up to see him smiling. He'd been fucking with me. "You're such a fucker. I was starting to think all that tattoo ink seeped into your brain," I said. "I thought I was the one who is supposed to have all the jokes."

Bear appeared next to King. "We're just filling in for you until after the surgery," he said, firing a text on his phone and shoving it back into his pocket.

"What surgery? What the fuck are you talking about?" I asked, wondering if I'd missed something.

"You know, the one to remove your head out of your ass," Bear said with a booming laugh.

I flicked him off. "I hope your kid doesn't inherit your dick-headedness, in fact, you better hope it doesn't get your looks either because you got nothing to offer in that department."

"I actually agree with you there. The more the kid gets from Ti the better," he said, looking less like the grumpy as fuck Bear I remembered and more like this weird happy guy who invaded his body. It was like watching one of those alien invasion shows and Bear was the product of some happy as fuck alien who decided to take up residence in his shirtless as fuck body. "But right now," Bear continued. "I need you to get your fucking ass up and come to the garage. We have something for you."

"What? Why?" I asked.

"Why? Because I fucking said so. Get up. Come on. Don't be a bitch," King said.

"I'll be there, give me one second." I pulled up the social networking site I'd been on when they'd interrupted me.

I'd told the truth when I told King I wasn't looking at porn. My dick hadn't exactly gotten the memo that I was alive just yet, but I had hopes for the fucker or else it was just a huge useless dead thing hanging between my legs about 60 years too fucking soon.

Glaring back at me from the computer screen was shiny black hair and dark almost black eyes. In her profile picture she was standing on dark sand behind grassy dunes, nothing like the beaches in the Logan's Beach area. It was a candid shot. She wasn't looking at the camera, instead she was looking off in the distance, the shadow of whoever took the picture was overlapping part of her face and immediately I hated whoever that motherfucker was who took the picture. Guy or girl. Maybe because it was obstructing me of a full view of her face or maybe it was because she looked so unguarded and I hated anyone who wasn't me who'd gotten to see her that way.

She didn't post that often. The sporadic pictures that were on her timeline were all dated several months apart.

I clicked on the ABOUT info section of her page.

"Come the fuck on!" King yelled out and thank God he was at the garage or my head would be swimming with the sound of his deep bellowing voice.

"Jesus fucking Christ you two!" I shouted back. Before I shutdown the computer I might have made Bear and King wait forty seconds more so I could hack into Dre's Facebook account and updated her relationship status.

To *married.*

I wasn't sure *why* the fuck I did it, but I was happy as fuck that I did. And when I walked out the front door and headed toward the garage to meet Bear and King it was with a big genuine fucking smile plastered all over my fucking face.

PREPPY

"God, I've fucking missed you, you're so fucking beautiful," I cooed, like I was talking to an infant. I lifted the triangle of broken mirror to eye level so I could get a more up close and personal look at the perfect lines of white powder, separated in picturesque rows on top of the glass. "Fuck, I think I'm tearing up… it's been too fucking long, but that's alright, we're gonna fix that, right now. We're gonna fix it so fucking good, baby."

"You gonna snort that shit or fuck it?" Bear asked and both he and King laughed reminding me that there were two others in King's studio besides me and the blow.

Bear was sitting on the floor with one leg pulled up so he could rest his elbow across it, his back against a bank of drawers that opened to one of King's many toolboxes. King sat on a rolling stool with his elbow propped up against a built in counter space set back in the wall, a beer to his lips. My blow and I were taking up space on the middle cushion of the black leather couch meant to be a waiting area for King's tattoo clients.

The studio was all brand new. Something King had put in when he rebuilt the garage and the garage apartment. It was small, but it was clean, and all the equipment was state of the art. A custom neon sign hung over the door on the inside. It was a skull wearing a crown and a bow tie. KING'S TATTOO that blinked from green to blue to red. With all the lights off inside the wall color change, reflecting a slightly different hue with every switch of the sign.

King had never needed to keep up the tattoo business, the money he made permanently marking the skin of bikers and spring breakers was only a fraction of what we made with the

Granny Growhouses plus the other shit we always had our hands in. But as I looked around at the framed pictures of the work that King had recently done, I knew that he kept it up because it was a part of him.

The same way I was gonna fuck up some blow. Because it was a part of me. Or at least, it was gonna be.

"Come to Daddy," I said. I held the rolled up bill to my nose and closed one nostril, leaning over I snorted up every last bit of the cocaine goodness. I sat back up, sniffling to make sure every last bit of white powdered goodness was as far up in my fucking brain as possible. I wiped my nose and it hit me harder than I ever remember it hitting.

The high was fucking incredible.

I felt invincible as Bear took the bill from my hand and snorted his own line. He passed it to King who shook his head and held up the joint he was smoking.

"Don't tell me you don't party anymore," I said. "You that pussy whipped where you can't do a little fucking blow with your long lost dead fucking friend? I mean, we're following all the rules right? It's after dark, the kids aren't home, and we're in your shop in the garage. Article FIFTEEN, LINE TWENTY SEVEN of all your new fucking rules clearly states that this is an acceptable time to get seriously fucked up."

"Nope, these days I just prefer to slow the fuck down instead of speed the fuck up. It's called relaxing in case you've never heard of it."

"Sounds fucking awful," I said, dumping more powder from the baggie onto the mirror. "Although whatever you've been doing has really upped your tatt game." I pointed to the collection of pictures on the wall. "Some of that shit is downright amazing man." I tipped my chin to one on the bottom. A sleeve on a woman's arm with light grey colors mixed with pinks and blues. "I mean that one's girly but still really fucking badass."

King laughed. "Ray did that one."

I knew she was assisting King and that she'd tattooed the bird on his hand, but I didn't know she was on that level.

"She's getting pretty fucking good," King said, beaming with pride.

"So I figure I can borrow your truck for now if that's alright with you, Boss-Man," I started, taking the joint he passed me. The blow putting into overdrive my lazy brain and for a few moments made me feel almost fucking normal.

Almost.

"I think I've got some cash buried somewhere just gotta remember where first, then I'll go into Dunn's over in Coral Pines and get my own ride, seeing as how my last one exploded and all."

"Why?" King asked like it was a far fetched idea.

"See, cars take you from point A to motherfucking point B," I pointed out. "Wait, you're the one who has a degree and Bear's the high school drop out, right? That's not something that's twisted up in my memory?

Bear laughed and King rolled over and kicked his foot.

"How the fuck else am I gonna get to the GG's to inspect and collect?" They paused their little tickle slap and I didn't miss the concerned look that passed between them.

"Preppy, you don't have to go back to work. We only have three or four left of the GG houses anyway. I got Billy working them for now, plus Ray helps out. There's no rush."

"Billy? Like chef Billy?"

"That's the one. His place got flooded a few months back and until the insurance kicks in he's been helping out here and there," King explained.

Bear scratched his neck. "Yeah, man. So you can relax for a hot second. Heal. Take some fucking time for yourself."

I shook my head. "I've spent too much time alone thinking. I don't need to do it anymore. I'm fucking ready." I stared them both down and wiped at my nose. "Are you gonna tell me that I'm not?"

"Preppy," King said, leaning forward and taking a long slow drag on his joint. "Ray needs the truck for the kids and I've got my bike, but Bear and I already talked about it and he's got a few rides around the club laying around we can get fixed up for you."

"Alright then," I said, snorting two more lines and lighting my own cigarette. "I missed drugs," I lamented. Cocaine may not be comforting to some people, but to me it was like meatloaf and apple pie.

It was home.

I looked up to the ceiling and then through the window of the backyard. "How the fuck did you afford this garage? The house being fixed up? Last I checked your finances solely revolved around getting Max back and that was more than any of us had combined."

King filled me in on the story, although I felt like it was more of the same deja-vu I felt with Thia when he was telling me about Ray's ex husband and Max and going to rescue her from the psycho.

"That didn't answer my question. How can you afford all this?"

Bear chimed in. "Because as it turns out, King didn't need

the money for Max. Senator man brought her back on his own accord. Then it seems that Ray came into some money. Like a lot of fucking money." Bear smiled, "So…"

"Boss-man," I said, turning my attentions to him. He was already rolling his eyes. "You've got a sugar mama?"

"Go fuck yourself, prep," King said although he was laughing when he said it. He took the bottle of whiskey from Bear and poured a long stream down his throat before passing it to me.

I was still swallowing when Bear sat up from the toolbox. He looked at me with a serious look on his face. A look I wanted to avoid because serious looks came with serious questions and I wanted nothing to do with those. "Prep, I gotta ask you. The girl. The one who came to see you. I remembered her from back in the day. I thought she was a BBB or something but that doesn't seem right either."

"Or something," I shrugged, taking another shot from the bottle. I passed it back to Bear.

"Prep, I've known you since we were stupid and young, now that I'm older and a little less stupid, I know there's more to this story then you're telling me 'cause there ain't no fucking way a BBB would be comin' round here unless it was to knife you in your sleep."

"I'd like to hear this too," King said, leaning forward onto his knees.

"Ain't much to say," I lied. "You might know her a lot better than you think you do," I said to Bear.

Like backdoor better.

"Well if she was a club girl then yeah, of course I know her. And I recognized her right away when she came over to the house. I just can't remember her around the club, or being at the parties with the other BBB's."

"She wasn't a BBB. She was…a girl who hung around," I tried to explain without going into too much detail, growing more and more frustrated with the fucking inquisition.

"A friend…who you were fucking?" King asked.

I sighed and leaned my elbows on my knees. "You'd just got sent away," I said to King. "And Bear was out on that long ass ride to wherever. Grace was in the treatment center. Dre came around strung out on H." I smiled at the memory. "She tried to rob one of my GG's. Turned out to be her grandmother's house. Mirna. She stuck around. Helped me with some shit I needed help with. Then she left. That was all there was to it." I shrugged and passed the bill to Bear who snorted two lines off the table. His dark blue eyes were open wide, bright, and clear as fuck. "Not a fucking big deal," I added.

"Prep, this girl came back after years out of nowhere, and then the wife thing," Bear said like he was trying to prove a point. "We don't know this chick. She could be involved in all this somehow. Part of the master plan that kept you locked up for Chop. Maybe if you tell us more. Tell us exactly what happened down there," he pushed.

"No fucking way," I said.

"Preppy, if you tell us then…" King started.

"Listen," I cut him off. I pointed between the two of them. "I know you two are looking to find out what happened to me. To see who else was in on it or who helped Chop cover up the fact that I was still alive. I get that we need to figure out who else might have had their hands in this so we can wipe them from the face of the fucking planet, but put your fucking detective hats away for one second here. The girl, Dre, she isn't trying to scam you or kill me or anything like that. She didn't have a part in any of Chop's crazy shit. I called her my wife when I was coming to because I was coming out of a motherfucking coma. I mean, I saw this video once on MeTube where the guy was waking up from dental surgery and thought his wife was Mother Teresa, started praying to her and everything."

King leaned forward against his hands on the back of the sofa across from me. "Tell me something, this new look of yours got anything to do with this chick coming back around?"

"How the fuck do you know she was back around?"

King raised his eyebrows as if I should already know. I did.

"Ray," I muttered.

King nodded.

Not being able to sit in one spot any longer I stood up and paced in front of the couch. "No, this ain't got shit to do with her," I answered, and it was the truth. How would I even go about telling my friends that I shaved my head and face bald because I hated looking at myself only to find that I hated the shaved version of me even more? They'd been through so much thinking I was dead. The last thing they needed was to bare my fucking burdens as well.

That's why I was never going to tell them everything that happened with Chop.

Never.

They both eyed me skeptically. I was about to explain further that they didn't need to worry about Dre when Bear's eyes lit up. "Fuck, I remember her now. I remember talking to you about her. Her dad was looking for her or something like that…" his face lit up in a huge smile and I wanted to both smile back and punch him in the god damned face when I realized what memory he was recalling. "How the fuck did I almost forget that?"

"Forget what?" King asked.

Bear scrunched up his forehead as he tried to recall the memory. "I can't remember all the details, but it was here. A party I think."

"Yeah, sounds about right," I said.

"You had her…here?" King asked.

"Why is that so strange? We had all sorts of bitches at our parties."

Bear's smile grew even brighter and I froze, knowing exactly what he was about to say because I saw the memories taking hold in that brain of his. "'Cause this is the only bitch we both had our dicks in at the same time."

I could have said a million things but instead I chose to change the subject. "So when are we having my homecoming party?" I asked.

"You ready for that?"

"I'm ready for anything," I said, snorting another line and hoping the blow would help me believe my own lie.

CHAPTER ELEVEN

DRE

THE HOUSE ITSELF felt the same but looked a little different. The garage had either been remodeled or replaced because even in the dark it looked brand new. The main house had a new coat of paint for sure. The numerous windows are clean and appear to have new white window frames. The soffit that had been rusting and falling down were all new as well. The space under the house that used to be cluttered with random broken parts was completely clear of junk and was now being used as parking. The truck that Ray had driven when she came to see me at Mirna's took up the space on the far wall. Several motorcycles took up the rest.

Torches with bright flames burned along the front walkway. All the lights were glowing from the bottom story, but only a single light was on upstairs, the window glowing yellow before whoever was in that room, that VERY familiar room, abruptly shut the blinds.

"This was a really bad idea," I whispered to Brandon who wraps his arm around my shoulder. "I shouldn't have come." I turned back around but Brandon grabbed me by the wrist.

"You're here now, Dre. You came to sell the house and get

closure right? Well," he said, gesturing to the house. Laughter, along with the light thump from the beat of the music playing echoed from the backyard. I knew where Brandon was about to say and he must have saw that I knew because he never finished his sentence. Instead, he took my hand and pulled me toward the house. I could've argued but there was no point. I hated it when he was right, which was often. I tried to relax my stiff shoulders by taking a deep calming breath and exhaling slowly.

Nope, didn't work.

"Hey, over here" Ray shouted, spotting us from the porch, waving her arms around in the air. "I'm so glad you made it," she said, approaching us. With Ray was the same beautiful girl with strawberry blonde hair who was there the day I discovered that Preppy was alive. "This is Thia," Ray introduced.

"You can call me, Ti," she offered with a sweet smile. My eyes dropped to the humungous baby belly between us. "Yeah, I know, I'm huge," Ti said when she saw where I was looking. She patted her belly. "Any day now though and this little munchkin will finally stop stomping on my bladder. I swear to Christ I feel like the baby is using my pelvis as a trampoline. Up and down and up and down. I'm in shock I haven't split in two yet." I could feel how uncomfortable she was. Beads of sweat appeared on her pale skin, spotting over the bridge of her nose and cheeks. She fanned herself with her hand. "Is it hot out here? I feel like it's really hot."

It was the coolest night since I'd arrived in Logan's Beach, although that meant it was in the seventies so to a pregnant woman that had to still be borderline surface of the sun temperature.

"I'm Brandon," Brandon offered, shaking Ti's hand.

"Shit, I'm sorry. I forgot to introduce you again," I apologized.

"No worries, I know you have a lot on your mind." Brandon gave my shoulder a squeeze and didn't let go. He turned toward Ray and Thia. "Ladies, I think this one here could use a drink."

"Yes!" Ray said, holding up her own beer dripping with condensation. Thia looked at it lovingly. Like it was an old friend she missed dearly. I tried not to laugh, hiding my smile behind my hand. "I'll show you where the coolers are," Ray said, hooking her arm with mine. She led me away from Brandon who offered to help Thia back up the steps into the house to find Bear.

Ray showed me where the coolers were against her house in the back. There was a crowd of people in all forms of sitting, standing, and leaning, around the bonfire in the backyard. The smell of cigarette smoke and weed hovered in the still night air. Ray reached into one of the coolers and twisted off the top of a beer, she handed it to me.

I took a sip of the bubbly liquid, scanning the crowd before me. I told myself I wasn't looking for HIM, but I knew it was a lie. I would also have been lying to myself if I said that the tight high waisted black pencil skirt I was wearing that hugged my hips and ass wasn't for him. Neither was the fitted blue polka dotted tank top with the heart shaped bra cups that pushed my cleavage up to unbelievable limits. Neither was the hour I spent curling my hair into perfect barrel curls and trimming my bangs to fall just right off to the side. Or the bright red on my lips or the dab of perfume behind my ears.

So even if it WAS for him. It was for me too.

It had been a long time since I'd dressed in the pin-up style that I loved so much, but the second my foot hit the ground on Logan's Beach soil I felt a need to wear the clothes I loved to feel more connected to the place I loved. I rarely wore jewelry but

I'd slipped on my grandmother's tiny diamond engagement ring that my grandpa had given to her when he proposed and she'd given to me when I was still just a kid and couldn't appreciate it like I did now. I'm glad my dad had it tucked away in a safety deposit box and given it to me as a gift after I completed rehab, because there was no doubt if I'd had it earlier that I would have pawned it at some point during what I started to refer to in my head as THE DARK YEARS.

I didn't spot Preppy but I instantly recognized Billy, the chef who cooked the crab Preppy and I had caught. It wasn't hard to spot him, it's not like I could miss him. He was almost seven feet tall, standing at least a head taller than most of the crowd and the bulk of his body was massive. The jean overalls he wore without a shirt underneath wasn't exactly an outfit that blended in either. He stood at the very back of the crowd, a mason jar to his lips.

I tapped my foot to the Kane Brown song playing over the speaker perched on the bottom step of the back porch and pretended like I was relaxing when in reality I felt like my airway was tightening, cutting off my ability to breath with each passing second.

King came over to us, tipped his head to acknowledge me, and grabbed her by hand, dragging her off without saying a word.

Very caveman, I thought.

Very fucking hot.

Thia found Bear because I spotted them standing by the bonfire where King had pushed his way to the front, pulling Ray behind him but I didn't see Brandon anywhere.

Suddenly I felt an awareness course through my body. It hit me so hard my nipples tightened under my shirt. I knew exactly who I was going to see when I turned around toward where I felt the pull rippling through the air. I held my breath. I knew he'd be there.

But I wasn't prepared for how I felt when I saw him.

Sweaty palms. Rapidly beating heart. A feeling of excitement and panic all at the same time.

It was just like when I started using heroin. Right before I plunged the needle in my arm there was a feeling almost as good as the high itself.

The anticipation. The fear.

I knew deep inside that it didn't matter how prepared I was to see him, because I'd never be prepared for the way Preppy made me feel.

The second I spotted him in the crowd I knew that this wasn't going to be some sort of warm and fuzzy reunion.

No, it was a fucking relapse.

CHAPTER TWELVE

PREPPY

"NOT THIS FUCKING guy again!" a high pitched feminine voice behind me shouted, a girl of blonde hair flashed in front of my eyes but I didn't need to see her face to know who the source of that annoying voice was.

I turn around and I'm face to face with Rage. Literally the only living person on the planet who knows how to push every button I have by just existing. Also, she was the only hot chick on the planet who might as well not have a vagina because there was nothing about her that myself or little Preppy liked. NOTHING. "Oh my shit! Who invited Suzie Home-Killer to the party?" I asked outlaid. "Don't you have puppies to off or something, Rage? Should I hide the coyote so you don't stake it in the heart for shits and giggles?"

She pointed at me with her beer bottle. "For your information that fucking coyote loves me and so does Thia so behave yourself if you know how to. Oh, and I'm glad to see you ditched the ugly bow tie," she said, pointing to the collar of my t-shirt. "It was a *dead* trend."

I pursed my lips. "That's funny, especially when I'm pretty sure everyone you've ever met becomes a dead trend at some point."

She cocked her head to the side. "Well then I wouldn't stand too close if I were you," she said, taking a step forward.

I took a step toward her in challenge. "Doesn't bother me. Haven't you heard? I've already been dead."

She laughed and if you didn't know she was satan anyone else would take it as a genuine laugh like I'd just told a funny joke. "That's right, I forgot to ask you," she made a show of clearing her throat. "Hey loser, do anything fucking stupid lately? You know, like getting captured and tortured? I mean, for the record I'm glad you're back from the dead by the way, if anything just so I can make fun of you for being stupid enough to get killed in the first place."

I scoffed. "Oh yeah? You think getting killed is stupid? I'm not the one who throws a fucking temper tantrum and all of a sudden a city block falls to the streets."

Rage rolled her eyes. "OMG it was like two buildings at the most."She paused. "That time." She smiles in a sly way that tells me that she's still proud of the work she's done.

"As pleasant as ever, Rage," I said, stepping back and taking a swig of my beer, searching the suddenly empty lawn for anyone to talk to other than Genghis Rage.

"Well, I can't say I'm not disappointed to see you amongst the living again," she said, buffing her french manicured nails on her hot pink t-shirt that read NO FUCKS GIVEN.

I looked at her right in her cold dead blue eyes. "Funny, I'm deliriously happy I'm alive but standing here right now, looking at you, it's the first time I'm kind of fucking wishing I was still dead too. You know, but not as dead as your soul."

She smiled wickedly. "I've always loved your compliments,

Samuel," she sang whimsically, batting her lashes for a beat before returning the disapproving frown to her face.

"Almost as much as I love thinking about how they're going to cast your episode of "Making of a Serial Killer."

"If you want to be dead again just say the fucking word and it can be arranged," she spat, squaring her feet.

"You wanna go, bitch?" I said, jumping back on my heels and raising my fists like a boxer. "'Cause we can go right now."

"With pleasure," Rage said. She was about to set her beer down in the grass when a voice interrupted us.

"That's enough, kids," said a tall biker who put his arm around Rage. I waited for her to push him off and jump back into wanting to fight me mode but her entire demeanor softened at his touch and surprisingly she didn't even flinch.

"Oooooh. I see that Bomber Barbie has found herself a Ken?" I asked looking from Rage to the biker.

"Watch it," the guy warned, protectively standing in front of Rage who stood on her tiptoes and scowled over his shoulder before stepping out in front of him.

"It's good to see that Rage isn't dead inside like we'd thought for so long. Hi, I'm Preppy," I said extending my hand.

"Nolan," the man offered with a shake and a small smile that told me he was trying his hardest not to laugh. Another biker in a matching cut walks up and hands Nolan a beer, he puts his arms over his shoulder and they huddle together, whispering what my guess would be about stupid biker bitch shit.

"Speaking of people who's souls you murder, where's Smoke?" I asked. Smoke was her mentor and a fuck of a tracker. I was only asking because I'd already heard that he'd left town for good and it was in some way her fault although I didn't know all the details.

She shrugged and the angry V lines in her forehead straightened out. "Got no clue these days," she said, putting her hands in her back pockets and rocking back on her heels.

"Hopefully far a fucking way," Nolan said through his gnashed teeth, chiming in over his shoulder.

"Nolan," she warned, taking a much softer tone I'd ever heard her use before but Nolan was already back to his conversation with the other biker.

"O.M.G. You're dick whipped! I whispered, pointing to Nolan. Aren't you? Wow, this is fucking amazing. Tell me, was it his cock or the fact that he doesn't murder babies in their sleep that made you go from Ted Bundy to Teddy Bear? Tell me, are you planning on doing that whole black widow thing where you get close to them before slitting their throats in their sleep one by one? Cause I'm not gonna lie, that's a pretty cool fucking plan."

"I'm not a character in a comic book, asshole. And I don't kill babies," she snarled. "And I don't kill anyone in their sleep. That's just…rude."

I shrugged and took another sip of my beer. "Whatever you tell yourself so you can sleep at night. Or wait, DO YOU sleep now or are you still hanging from the ceiling like a fucking bat?"

Rage glared at me without answering but the glare said it all. If looks could kill. Well, they didn't need to because SHE could kill.

I reached in my pocket for my smokes and lit one. Rage made a show of waving the smoke out of her face although it was nowhere near her. "You do sleep? Wow, it's like I don't even know you anymore. Tell me, what are the other main differences between the raging bitch you were and the raging bitch you've become?" I crossed my arms over my chest and leaned in like I couldn't wait to hear her answer.

"Fuck off, *Preppy*."

"Oh come on, Rage. You can do better than that. I mean it's just so nice to see that you've settled down and with a BIKER no less. I really had no idea that you were home knitting scarves and planning babies. I apologize for everything I've said, Rage," I offered, raising my hands in mock surrender. She flipped me off. "It's totally cool that you're barefoot in the kitchen. Feminism is for the birds and all that. Oh shit, does this mean you're gonna be the soccer mom?"

"What about you?" she asked, pointing to the kids running around in the yard. "Doesn't exactly look like you're all alone here."

"Yeah, well, still feels like I am," I muttered, offering that bit of truth since we were all being honest with our hatred and all.

"I know all too well what you mean," she said, looking up to Nolan who was still deep in conversation.

"Did we just agree on something?" I asked with a shake of my head and a tinge of disgust in my voice. "Listen, the universe is already fucked up. We don't need this kind of karma in our lives."

"No, we did not agree on anything," she argued. "I was just saying how fucking boring your life is and then I wanted to add how shitty you look after a few months of mild torture." She leaned in and whispered. "I bet you screamed like a bitch," she pulled back and took a sip of her beer.

A part of me. A part deep DEEP down part of me liked that Rage had no filter and said whatever was on her mind. It was refreshing in a way because everyone else seemed to be walking on fucking eggshells around me and in a way Rage was right. It was getting really fucking boring.

"Is that what Nolan does?" I asked with a wink. "Does he make you scream like a bitch or do you just pull out your cock and compare who's is bigger?"

I could hear her audibly growl and then sigh heavily. "Well, Preppy, it's been real. Until we're forced together in the same social situation again, which hopefully isn't any fucking time soon," she said clinking the neck of her beer to mine with a fake smile plastered on her face that dropped before she even turned back around. She stomped passed Nolan, catching his attention, his head spinning in her direction while she muttered, "Pussy, can't take torture like a fucking man."

I responded with a muttering of my own, "Aeropostale Assassin."

"You know," I said to Nolan whose buddy had just walked off toward the house. "Sometimes I think the reason she's so hot is because of that flaming poker shoved up her ass."

Surprisingly, Nolan chuckled instead of punching me in the face as he watched Rage stalk off, his focus primarily on her swaying ass. "Hot. Yeah, she most definitely is," he said, biting his bottom lip and rocking his weight from one leg to the other. "I ummmm… I gotta go…" his words trailed off as he chased after Rage who I'm sure was on her way toward whatever circle of hell she usually crawled into to seek solace from her bruised ego.

I took a deep drag of my cigarette. In a way Rage and I hating each other was the most normal thing I'd experienced since I'd been back and for a brief moment I felt a little better. Slightly lighter. Like all wasn't right with the world, far fucking from it, but maybe, just MAYBE it could be.

Someday.

I felt so good that I almost believed my own lie and that to me was progress.

It also might have been the blow.

Blow or progress, either way I was starting to feel pretty fucking good.

That is until I tipped up my beer up to my mouth and caught a glimpse of a feminine figure through the green glass of the bottle. A figure, although distorted and blurred, the orange glow of the burning torches glowing on both sides of her, I would recognize anywhere. I kept the bottle to my lips a full thirty seconds after I'd drained it, thinking that what I was seeing was a figure of my imagination as it had cruelly been so many times before. Slowly, I lowered the bottle and I was able to see her clearly for the first time in a long time.

My breath hitched in my throat. She was still the most beautiful woman I'd ever seen.

Dark hair, short tight skirt, and bright red fuckable lips.

My wife was home.

"ATTENTION EVERYONE," KING said, standing on wooden bench butted up against the brick edge surrounding the bonfire pit. The flames rose at least five feet above his head. He reached down and pulled Ray up to stand with him on the bench. Even in the dark I could see her face turning bright red with embarrassment as she hid her face in her hands, peering out through the spaces between her fingers before covering back up again. King pulled her hand from her face and took it in his own. He held up a bottle of whiskey to the party-goers who had all gathered around to hear what he had to say. Public speaking wasn't exactly King's thing. SPEAKING wasn't exactly his thing, but as he looked down at Ray and spoke to the crowd there were none of the mutters or grunts that I remembered King using to communicate. In fact, the motherfucker was downright articulate, albeit I detected a tad bit drunk as well.

"We have a lot to celebrate tonight," he started, his eyes scanning the crowd until they met mine. "The first thing being that my best fucking friend in the world has come back from the fucking dead!" He took a swig from his bottle and raised it in the air, pointing it toward me and I did the same.

The crowd clapped and screamed, their voices swirling around me like a tornado of noise, pushing me back and forth. I wobbled on my feet, trying to stay upright. I was about to fall over when King raised his hands and got the crowd to die down, oblivious of the state I was in. I opened and closed my mouth, moving my jaw around in an attempt to get my ears to pop but it wasn't working. Nothing was working. I was a prisoner to the noise that assaulted me like toxic arrows shot into my fucking eardrums. "The second thing we have to celebrate is that now that I have my best men here with me. My family. It feels right now. So Ray and I here are getting married in two weeks right here and you are all better be coming to our fucking wedding!"

The crowd erupted even louder than before and I felt like a cannon had exploded next to my ear. King picked up Ray who wrapped her legs around his waist as he kissed her for all to see, claiming her with his mouth. Someone whistled from behind me, the sound piercing through my skull. My vision shifted from blurry to clear then back again. I swayed on my feet. When the attention was off of me I stumbled through the crowd toward the house, tripping over people who probably thought I was just drunk as I barreled through them like a blind bull charging.

The world was spinning. I covered my one ear with one hand and felt for the wall of the house with the other. A pair of hands grabbed my shoulders and my fight instincts kicked in. I shook them off and jumped back, raising my fist in the air. It was then my eyes chose to focus again, but the pressure behind them was unbearable. I looked the ground at tiny feminine bare feet with red toe-nail polish. I traveled up bare calves to the black skirt that stopped right below her knees and I nodded, trying to let her know she could guide me. She got the message and again touched my shoulders. I flinched but realized as her hand slid down my arm and she guided me to the front of the house. Away from the crowd. Away from the noise. Away from the nightmare that both of those things brought me time and time again.

"I was lost," I said, breathlessly, not exactly sure what I was trying to say, although Dre seemed to understand. She gripped my arm tighter.

"You were, but I found you."

DRE

"Just give me a minute," Preppy said, breathing heavily. He leaned back against the thick trunk of a huge banyan tree on the far corner of the front yard. The furthest away we could get from whatever it was that had caused Preppy to break down in the middle of the party. He was rubbing his eyes and temples, wincing and baring his teeth.

"Are you in pain?" I asked. "Where?" I looked him over and couldn't see anything obvious. No tears in his hoodie or jeans, no blood stains of any kind. In fact, besides how he was responding to whatever it was causing him such distress, he looked good. REALLY good.

He'd filled out since I'd seen him last. His cheeks weren't nearly as hollow as before. His face was no longer clean shaven and was a few days past being able to call it 'stubble.' Where the hair on his head was always a few shades lighter than his face, as it grew they looked to be a perfect match, both being a lighter shade of brown. His hazel eyes weren't as glazed over but they still look unfocused.

"I'm fine!" Preppy said, blinking rapidly several times. He looked up at me.

He was anything but fine.

Just when I thought he was calming down he grabbed the sides of his head and dropped to his knees in the grass. "Aaaagggrrrrrr," he yelled as if something inside was clawing it's way out.

I knelt down beside him, unsure of how to help him especially since I didn't know what it was that was hurting him so badly.

Distraction, I thought. So I did the only thing I could think of. I got right in Preppy's face, I grabbed his shoulders… and I pressed my mouth to his. At first his entire body jumped like I'd stung him but at least he'd stopped screaming. I didn't do a damn thing. I went perfectly still and waited as I felt his entire body relax, his lips soften against mine. A tingling bolt of desire hummed in my clit as I pressed my chest against his, packing him up against the tree.

He pulled back just far enough to speak, "What the fuck was that?" he asked, his cool breath against my lips as he panted against me. His pupils were wide and dark, barely any of his beautiful hazel eyes were visible. Wherever he'd gone, he'd come back.

"Distraction?" I asked, sounding breathless.

"Huh?" he asked, making no move to push me away.

"Distraction," I said, suddenly second guessing myself and thinking that maybe I'd done the wrong thing after all. "When I was little and I broke my arm falling out of a tree I was climbing, my dad, he distracted me when the doctor was putting the cast on. He jumped around the ER making these loud monkey noises." I laughed at the memory. "I thought he was insane until I realized the cast was on and I hadn't felt a thing."

"So that kiss was meant to be a distraction?" Preppy asked, amusement dancing in his eyes. He leaned in closer and my nipples pebbled in awareness. My panties were damp as he grabbed my arms and ran his hands down to my hips and around to my ass.

I nodded.

"Well then Doc," he said, running the backs of his knuckles down my cheek and jaw. I leaned into his touch. "I think we can do better than that."

I was about to ask him what he meant when his lips met mine. It was nothing like the first kiss which was practical and tight lipped. It was soft and hard all at the same time. He molded his mouth to me, his tongue connecting with mine in a way that made me feel a vibration between my thighs, like his tongue was licking right at the entrance of my pussy. I moaned into his mouth as he gripped the back of my head and held me in place as he assaulted me with his mouth, and I opened for him.

I heard something in the distance. My name being called?

But I was too far gone to care, too lost in the high that was Samuel Clearwater to care who needed me or why.

Because I needed that kiss that moment and I was going to take it while I could.

"Dre!" Brandon shouted. Preppy pulled back and we both looked into the yard where Brandon was frantically searching for me.

"Who the fuck is that?" Preppy asked, holding me against him tighter.

"Brandon." No sooner had I said it that Brandon spotted us and started jogging our way.

"Brandon?" Preppy asked, we were both breathing hard, my nipples rubbing against his chest and the fabric of my tank top as we breathed in the same air. "Who the fuck is *Brandon*?" he asked. That's when he looked down between us, his eyes grew furious. His arms stiffening. I glanced down to see what he could be looking at and that's when I saw Mirna's ring on my finger, the diamond glistening against the reflection of the moon.

Preppy growled and let me go abruptly, side stepping me, and without him to hold onto and my thighs shaking with weakness I fell against the tree. He met Brandon halfway between the yard and the tree but before I realized what his intentions were his fist was flying and Brandon was flailing on the ground, clutching his bloody nose.

"Preppy!" I called out, but he'd already disappeared into the crowd. I ran to Brandon and started helping him up. "Come on, let's go get you some ice."

"Fuck," Brandon moaned, standing with a wobble and holding onto my shoulder. "Was that who I think it was?" he asked.

"Yeah, it was."

"Well I think your boyfriend just broke my fucking nose," Brandon said sounding like he was speaking through a drive through window at a fast food restaurant.

"He's not my boyfriend," I argued as I led him over to the coolers for some ice. I reached in and grabbed a few cubes, wrapping them in a napkin and pressing it to his face. He hissed. "Actually, I think he saw my grandmother's ring and thought you gave it to me."

Brandon started laughing. Full out belly laughing. "Oh my shit I have to call Ralph right fucking now," Brandon said reaching into his pocket for his phone.

"Why?"

"Because, your boyfriend thinks I'm straight. Who better to appreciate the humor in that than MY boyfriend?" Brandon said. He smiled as his thumb clicked across the screen.

He had a point. The situation would probably be funny to me.

Someday.

Brandon was just about to hold the phone up to his ear when the crowd erupted in cheers once again. I looked to where Thia and Bear were in the front and he was planting a big kiss on her mouth.

"Preppy, you're fucking next!" someone shouted, and I realized it was Billy. His mason jar now only half of what it had been ten minutes before. "Don't drink the water over here or you'll be getting hitched!"

At the sound of his name my stomach flipped. Brandon had finished dialing and was holding the phone to his ear. I heard Ralph on the other end saying "Hello? Baby is that you?"

Brandon opened his mouth and was about to speak but stopped when someone on the other side of the crowd chimed in.

"Actually, I got married before these two beautiful big fucks," the voice slurred.

Preppy.

The crowd was quiet. A few people in the front shuffled around and parted and that's when I saw him again. This time he was standing on the edge of the fire pit where Bear was standing only seconds before. "In fact, my wife's here tonight," Preppy said. He looked around and spotted me with Brandon. Our eyes locked and he pinned me in place with his gaze. He lifted the bottle in his hand in my direction. He swayed slightly. "This is for you, Doc. Isn't my wife beautiful folks?" I felt a hundred set of eyes shift toward me. "Don't worry about the bleeding guy. That's just my wife's finance who I just punched in the fucking face." He threw the bottle into the fire which cracked against the brick. Flames shot higher into the sky as he jumped down and disappeared from view.

Several people were calling out his name, including myself.

Brandon might have been the one Preppy hit, but I felt as if he'd punched me square in the gut.

CHAPTER THIRTEEN

PREPPY

LIFE WAS FUCKING loud.

And Doc was fucking engaged.

She kissed me.

Noise was everywhere and anywhere.

Whispers, laughter, chattering, music, tires on the gravel, birds in the trees. Even the low buzzing of King's tattoo gun in the next room had jack-hammer-esque quality to it that made my pulse pound in my head.

With each passing moment the noise grew louder and louder until I was face first on the mattress covering my head with a pillow and screaming into the sheets over the ear torture of every-day life.

I'd come to the apartment so that Doe, I mean RAY, and King's kid could have her room back but also because I thought it would be quieter.

I was wrong.

The last straw was a motherfucking cricket sitting just outside the open window. I jumped to my feet and darted from drawer to cabinet, discarding contents to the floor. I was so focused on my search I didn't hear Bear come in until he spoke up from the doorway. "Something I can help you look for?"

"My gun. Do you know where it is?" I asked without looking back at him. "Did you keep it or throw it away like the rest of my shit."

"Fuck you. We kept your shit for a long time and you know we don't throw away guns." Bear tilted his head. "You got someone to kill?"

"Fuck yeah I do," I corrected.

"You gonna tell me who?"

"Why is it all so fucking loud!" I shouted, opening the last cabinet in the kitchenette, pushing aside the pots and pans with no luck. I slammed the door and headed to the bedroom to start on my search there.

"Uhhhhh hear what?" Bear asked, following me into the bedroom and then the bathroom.

"Fuck, it," I finally said, giving up my search. I turned to Bear and held out my hand. "Let me use yours."

"First tell me who it is you thinking of killin'," Bear insisted, placing a protective hand inside his cut over his gun.

"You really don't hear that?"

Bear looked around and even briefly closed his eyes before opening them again. "I don't have a fucking clue what you're talking about."

"Close your eyes again. Fucking LISTEN," I snapped, growing frustrated. My mind racing.

The second Bear closed his eyes and removed his hand off his gun I reached inside his cut and before he could stop me I shot through the open window, blasting the little green bug into smithereens and in the process exploding the piece of faux marble covering the window sill and shattering the glass of the window when it fell from its locked position.

"Much better," I said, tossing the gun back at Bear before he had a chance to grab it back from me.

"You don't grab another man's gun, asshole," Bear growled, anger lacing his every word as I climbed back into bed. "What the fuck do you think you're doing?"

"Getting rid of some of the god-damned noise around here. That's what I was fucking doing."

"Preppy, you've lost your goddamned mind is what you've done," Bear barked over me. The door to the apartment slammed open and King burst into the room, a frantic look on his face.

"What the fuck was that?"

"Preppy sentenced a cricket outside the window to death by firing squad of one," Bear remarked.

"What the fuck is wrong with you?" King shouted, pulling me up and holding me in front of him, his face only inches from mine. An angry vein thrummed in his forehead as it had always done when he was pissed. I missed that vein.

"What the fuck is your problem?" I asked.

"Are fucking kidding me right now? My problem is that we have kids and women who fucking live here and you're firing a gun outside the god damned window like it's the wild west. Fuck, Prep. I know shit's different around here now, but that shit you just pulled wouldn't fucking fly before you went away either."

"I'm so fucking sorry that I don't live up to your new family man standards," I said, grabbing his wrist and tossing it away from where he had gathered a handful of my shirt in his hand. I grabbed a duffel bag from under the bed and tossed a few pairs of shorts and shirts into it.

"You need help?" King asked, his anger turning into frustration. "Do we need to send you somewhere? Just tell me what you fucking need, Preppy!"

"I need the noise to stop. I need the light to stop burning my fucking eyes. I need my fucking cock to work instead of lying limp between my fucking legs." I zipped the bag and tossed it over my shoulder. I looked back at King who was standing there with that look on his face that I was tired of seeing. "I need my friends to stop looking at me like I'm some dog who got hit by a fucking car."

"Where the fuck do you think you're going?" Bear asked as I made my way to the door.

"Somewhere much fucking quieter."

King's arm shot out, blocking me from the door.

"Just let him go," Bear said pulling on King's arm. He reluctantly let it fall with a growl and I left, slamming the door and leaving my two best friends behind me.

Nobody followed me.

Which was good.

Because I had no fucking idea where I was going.

CHAPTER FOURTEEN

KING

"HEY, YOU BUSY?" Pup asked, peeking her blonde head around the door.

"Just finishing up," I said, snapping off my black gloves and tossing them into the trash bin. I rolled my stool to the center of the room and she didn't need another invitation, she stepped into the room and between my legs so I could wrap my arms around her, but it wasn't close enough.

Never was.

I grabbed her hips and pulled her close until her body was firmly against mine and my face against her chest.

"What's going on?" I mumbled from between her tits. My last client just left and I was beat. It was the last session of six for one of the biggest and most intricate back pieces I'd ever done.

"Oh wow. It's beautiful," Pup exclaimed and when I looked up she had my phone in one hand and the other was covering her mouth as she looked down at the screen at the picture I'd just taken before I'd wrapped up his back and sent him on his way. "It's your best one yet."

"You say that about all of them," I said, again pressing my

face between her braless tits and wanting very badly to sleep there for the rest of the fucking night.

Pup laughed and stepped back but I wouldn't let her get far so I grabbed her hand and pulled her back into me. "I need to talk to you about something serious," she said.

"You pregnant again?" I asked, unable to hide the hope in my voice. Some may view my need to knock my woman up constantly as pathetic, but I saw her being pregnant with my baby as more than just carrying a kid. Her being pregnant with my baby was like the possession of her. A body and soul kind of thing. It made me rock fucking hard every time I thought of her belly growing and her tits swelling again.

"No!" she said, slapping me playfully on the shoulder. "We said we would take a break. We have three and I need a minute to just…to just breathe!"

"How long do you need to breathe baby?" I murmured, lightly running my teeth over sensitive spot of skin under her tit over her shirt. "A week?" I dug my fingers into her hips and moved my head lower to kiss the small strip of skin between her tank top and her shorts. "Two weeks?" I asked, licking a circle around her belly button. I looked up just as her pale cheeks turned bright pink. "Three? Because you know, baby, I'll give you whatever you want." I rubbed my thumbs over the tops of her thighs from the outside in, dipping them into the frayed opening of her shorts. Goosebumps rose on her warm flesh.

"Time," she said sternly. Well, as sternly as she could with my thumbs circling so close to her pussy. "I just want a little time."

"I'll give you two months," I bargained without waiting for her to reply. Instead, I watched as her eyes turn dark as I ran my nose over stomach and breathed in her arousal. There was no better scent on earth than my woman when she was turned on.

MY woman.

Something I could say a million fucking times and it never got old.

MINE.

"We…we can talk about that stuff. Baby stuff. La…later," she stammered. "Right now I need to talk to you. It's about Prep."

"What about Prep?" I asked, realizing that Pup was serious about whatever it was she had to talk to me about I needed some space so I could actually hear her so I took my tools over to the sink where I started taking apart my equipment for cleaning and sanitation.

Pup sighed and plopped down onto the black leather couch beside me, pulling her legs up onto the cushions and resting her chin on her knees. "He feels off to me. It all feels off."

King shrugged. "Everyone deals with shit their own way and he hasn't been around in a while. Let him ease back into things in his own way. He's gonna freak out now and again. He's been through some shit."

Pup sighed, her eyes looked tired. "I don't know how to say this to you so I'm just going to say it," she took a deep breath and looked at the floor when she said. "I don't think Preppy is telling the truth."

"About what happened to him?" I asked. "No fucking way. He's not saying much and that's understandable, but Bear's guys dragged him out of that hole themselves. There's no way he was lying about that."

She shook her head. "No, about the girl. About Dre. About who she is to him."

I shook my head, "Why would he lie about her?"

"Because don't you see? He lies to us because he doesn't want us to worry about him. He says he's fine when clearly he's not fine. If this girl meant something to him then he's keeping that to himself so we don't go trying to fix things for him."

I wiped off the last part of my tattoo gun, setting the tools in the sterilizer and hitting the button. Neon blue lights lit up the mini fridge looking contraption. A low hum vibrated from the machine. "Don't you think he deserves the benefit of the doubt? After all he's been through?" I turned around and leaned against the arm of the couch, towering over my girl.

"Yeah, I do. But..."

"What about after all WE'VE been through? I don't know about you, but I don't want to go digging into shit that don't need digging into just because a part of his story seems off to you. It's all fucking off. WAY fucking off. What matters is that he's home and he's got to deal with his shit when he's ready. Cut him some fucking slack, babe."

"I know, but he won't even talk about what happened to him," she said, looking down at her hands.

I tipped her chin up and I met her worried blue gaze. "He needs time. You feel me, Pup?"

"I feel you," she breathed, giving me that look that made my balls tighten every fucking time.

"Good," I said, leaning in to press my lips to hers and pushing down on her shoulders so that her back was against the cushions. I pushed her legs apart and quickly settled myself between them.

My favorite fucking place in the world.

"Now let's quit all the serious talk while I *seriously* fuck you until you're the one begging ME for another baby." I reached behind her and grabbed her ass, lifting her off the couch enough for my cock to press against her shorts covered pussy.

"I'll quit. I promise," she assured me, breathing heavy. "No more digging."

"Good girl," I said, palming her tits through her tank top, feeling her nipples harden underneath my touch had me impossibly hard and I was well on my way to fixing the situation she'd started the second she came into my shop wearing that little scrap of material she calls shorts and that impossibly tight top that did all sorts of everything for her already amazing body.

"I'll quit," she said again and I sensed we weren't done talking about it when she pushed against my chest until I had no choice but to set a knee on the floor so I could lift up off of her. "As soon as you take a look at this," she pulled a folded piece of paper from between her tits and I could give two shits if it was the declaration of independence or directions to the holy grail, all I could focus on was my need to tongue between her tits while I fingered her pussy from behind. "I dug this up a while ago. But I promise no more digging. Please," she begged, snapping my focus back up to her eyes.

It wasn't the kind of begging I was hoping for.

I rubbed my hand over my face and snatched the paper from her hands. She sat up next to me and watched as I unfolded it. It was a copy of some sort of official document. "What exactly the fuck is this?" I asked, looking down at some sort of photo copy of an official document. I mentally braced myself at what was to come because anything having to do with the law usually didn't end well.

At least, not for me it didn't.

Pup jabbed her finger at the paper. "Just keep going. Please," she insisted, her hands curled up around my bicep, her head against my shoulder as her lips silently moved as she read along with me. The smell of whatever girly shampoo she used wafted into my nostrils and did nothing to help reduce the massive hard on still pressing painfully against my jeans.

Focus.

I sighed, started at the beginning and then paused after reading the very first sentence. *No fucking way.* Not believing what I was reading I glanced from Pup back to the page and started all over again. Pup was no longer looking at the document, but at me as I read it again, this time out loud. "State of Florida, Division of Vital Statistics, Certificate of Marriage. Issued to Samuel Clearwater and Andrea Anne Capulet, issued this day, June the…" I paused and read the rest quickly, mumbling my way through the rest of the numerical facts with my hand over my mouth until I reached the bottom where the both the official seal of Florida and the County's stamp were right there on the bottom. "What did that girl say her name was?" I asked.

"Dre. Short for…"

"Andrea," I finished for her.

Pup nodded. "I showed this to Dre. She was surprised as hell. She said she was trying to help Preppy get Max by forging some documents to make Preppy seem more like an upstanding citizen but Preppy actually filed this with the clerk's office after she'd already left to go back home."

"Holy fuck. He did lie to me," I said, hating the way the words sounded coming from my own mouth and feeling bitter and hurt that my best friend, a man I saw as my brother could lie to me. "For YEARS he's been lying to me."

"So you don't care that he's married?"

"No, I don't fucking care. I mean, I don't know WHY but him getting married would never fucking bother me. What I fucking care about is that I was lied to by one of the only people on the planet I never thought I had to worry about lying to me!" I said, my voice rising along with my temper.

"You should talk to him. Ask him what it's all about. Maybe we can help him," Pup said.

"That's what I'm going to do," I said, stomping out the door with Pup close on my heels.

"What are you doing?" she asked, struggling to keep pace beside me as I stormed over to the main house.

"Going to get some answers," I replied.

"Wait!" Pup shouted, grabbing me by one of the belts on my arm. I stopped and turned around to face her. "We don't' even know where he is!"

Instantly my temper cooled at the reminder that we'd gone without him for so long. We fucking BURIED him for fucks sake and now we knew he was alive but didn't know where he was.

"We will find him. And then you will talk to him. I promise if that fucks things up more then we can talk about speeding up you getting me pregnant again." She pressed her soft lips to my neck and smell and nearness combination sent a shot of sensation directly to my already hardening cock.

"But what about right now?" I asked.

"Now?" She asked, growing bolder, slipping her hand into the back waistband of my jeans and cupping my ass. "Now we practice."

A growl tore from my throat as I lifted her up into my arms, her legs instantly wrapping around my waist. I felt the heat of her pussy against my cock as I walked with her into the shadows under the house and pushed her up against a pillar. "I'm particularly fond of this particular pillar," she cooed, tightening her legs around me.

"You make me fucking crazy woman," I said, grabbing her face in my hands and kissing her furiously. "You can bargain with me all you want, but you best remember who's in charge here." I squeezed her ass. "Of this," she arched her back against the pillar. "Of this," I said, pinching her nipple between my fingers. "Of this," I growled, shoving my hand down the front of her shorts and cupping her pussy in my palm. Her head dropped back as she rotated her hips, her body begging for more.

"More," she said, breathlessly.

I claimed her lips again, rocking rhythmically against the opening of her pussy, kissing her deeply and furiously, my tongue intertwining with hers in a way that made me ache to be balls deep inside of her.

It never mattered how many times I'd kissed Pup or even how many times I'd fucked her since we'd first met. None of that even mattered because it was as if time only made me want her more and more. I was sick with lust for her. A sickness I never wanted to be cured of. I pulled back for air and pushed a stray hair from her eyes, tucking it behind her ear. Her face flushed, her lips swollen and red. As soon as she spoke the last syllable of her question I entered her pussy in one long hard thrust that has me seeing stars as she squeezed around me like a fucking vice. She cried out and dug her fingernails into my shoulders.

Of course my phone rang right when I was about to drive home into my girl. It stopped but only to start back up again. Finally, Pup reached into my back pocket and handed it to me. I glared at her when I barked "What? We'll be right there," I said, clicking END on the phone and dialing Bear's number. I set Pup down on her feet and righted my jeans while waiting for him to answer.

"Who was that?" Ray asked, jogging beside me to keep up as I made my way to the garage where Bear had been tinkering around earlier.

I pounded on the door and it lifted seconds later, Bear stood there with a cigarette dangling from his mouth and a greasy wrench in his hand. I looked from Ray to Bear. "Billy called. He said Preppy came in screaming and knocking shit over at his crab shack. When Billy tried to settle him down he darted out the back. He can't find him anywhere and he just hopes…" I trailed off.

"What? He hopes what?" Ray asked, pulling at my shirt.

"That he didn't jump off the seawall."

CHAPTER FIFTEEN

DRE

WHEN THERE WAS a knock at the front door I assumed it was the realtor who was coming by to show a perspective buyer the house, but when I opened the door and saw Ray standing on my porch I was pleasantly surprised.

Well, I was pleasantly surprised until I realized what state she was in. Her eyes were red. She was twisting her hands together and bouncing nervously on the balls of her feet. King was standing outside of the truck in the driveway, an unreadable expression on his face? "Is he here?" Ray asked, glancing over my shoulder into the house.

"Who?" I asked.

"Preppy!" Ray shouted, pushing passed me and ran through the empty house, darting from room to room. She ran out just as quick as she'd run in and shook her head at King who clenched his fists and pounded them against the roof of the truck. His head dropped.

Ray ran to the truck and King got in the driver's seat.

"Wait! What's wrong?" I asked, running after them, feeling a sense of dread building inside of me.

They ignored me. King threw the truck in reverse. They'd

gotten about three feet down the driveway when I jumped behind the truck and held up my hands. King slammed on the brakes to avoid hitting me. "What the fuck. Get out of the fucking way!" King said, sticking his head out the window.

To say that King was frightening was the understatement of the century. The man was downright terrifying, but there was no way in hell I was letting them leave. "I'll move when you tell me what the fuck is going on and why you're searching my house and asking me if he's here."

King threw the truck in park and got out. He slammed the door and stormed up to me in a few long strides. He glared down at me and I could feel the anger in his gaze. "You need to get out of the fucking way," he seethed.

I shook my head and although my hands were shaking there was no way I was moving. "No. You'll have to run me over first. Tell me what the fuck is going on," I said, standing my ground.

King opened his mouth to speak but Ray appeared next to him, took his hand in hers and beat him to it. "Preppy freaked out and bolted. Can't find him anywhere. Thought he might have come here." Ray paused and looked to the floor. "He's not in a great place right now, and we're worried that he might have done something…stupid."

King let go of her hand and they both got back in the truck. I stepped out of the way with a sinking heart, watching them roll away when suddenly it hit me. I bolted to the passenger side and threw open the door of the truck. Again, King was forced to slam on the brakes. "What the hell are you doing?" Ray squealed as I jumped inside, forcing her to slide to the middle.

I closed the door and turned to a very confused and worry looking King and Ray. "I know where he is."

King called Bear on the way and told him where to meet us. After only a few minutes Bear appeared behind us on his bike, the roar of the engine rattling the rearview mirror as he followed us down the road.

It wasn't until we'd cleared the fence and the tall pine trees that we realized the moon wasn't the only thing lighting up the water tower.

Parked in the field below was an array of flashing red and blue from a fire truck, several police cars…and an ambulance.

CHAPTER SIXTEEN

DRE

THE HOSPITAL WAS a damn madhouse. Doctors and nurses pushed by, flying down the hallway at inhuman speeds like white-coated superheroes, shouting out complicated series of orders to one another that sounded nothing like words I'd ever heard in the English language before.

Everything in the place blinked and beeped and when the occasional alarm would sound more white coats would stampede toward the ER doors, their stethoscopes swinging from their necks like elephant trunks.

The waiting room was jam packed, every seat was taken as the nurses at the desk called out numbers like the deli counter at the grocery store. The hallways were lined with people, all in varying states of worry, who all tried to become a part of the walls to make room for the medical teams when they rolled another patient through. The smell of the place was sickening, like open sores and antiseptic. My stomach rolled.

"We need to see Samuel Clearwater, he's back there. What room is he in? How is he doing?" King demanded. The front desk nurse, looked as if she was about to argue until she glanced up from her computer between King and Bear. She looked back down to the screen. "He doesn't have a room yet. He's in an evaluation curtain."

"Where is the evaluation area?" Bear asked.

She shook her head. "Nuh, uh, you can't go back there unless you're immediate family."

"We're the closest thing to family he's got," Ray argued.

"Unfortunately, in this hospital that's not close enough. I'll send a doctor out with an update as soon as we have one. I suggest you take a seat until then. If and when he gets a room you can go back one at a time, but for now you have to wait like everyone else."

"Fuck this," King roared, heading toward the double doors marked DO NOT ENTER in large determined strides.

"Sir!" The nurse exclaimed throwing her tiny body in front of King before he reached his destination. She flipped her braids over her shoulders again and that's when I got a clear view of her name tag. IVY. And Nurse Ivy apparently had a huge set of balls on her to stand up against the likes of King. "Don't you make me call security up in here and have you thrown out. Because then you'll have to call for an update from your jail cell instead of sitting patiently in the waiting room like I so nicely asked you to do."

"Listen, Darlin'," Bear said, smiling down at Ivy who looked even less impressed with his attempt at a softer approach, although the lines in her forehead did decrease just a fraction. She was a female after all and Bear's slow southern drawl sounded like a deep purr. The kind that vibrated all the way through you to the ground. "Our friend in there. He hates hospitals more than anything. All I'm asking that you let one of us to go in there and check on him, really quick, just to make sure he's alright, and then we'll get out of your fucking hair." Nurse Ivy folded her arms over her chest, her determination to keep them out unwavering.

Two uniformed guards approached King and Bear. "Ma'am, please," Bear pled, as the guards stepped between them and Ivy. "He needs someone back there with him and he doesn't have any immediate family here."

"Yes, he does!" I shouted a bit too loudly. Not only did King, Bear, and Ray turn to face me, but so did the nurse, the guards, and most of the waiting room. "I can go back there with him. I'm his immediate family."

"Sure you are, Miss," the nurse said with a roll of her eyes. "And who exactly are you? His sister? No wait, his mama?"

I had about all I could take of the bitch. I stepped between King and Bear. "No, I'm his WIFE," I growled.

She looked up to King and Bear. "No immediate family, huh?" she said with her lips pursed. "You unaware that your friend had a wife?" she asked skeptically.

"It's complicated," Ray clarified.

"Take me to my husband. Now," I said to the nurse, pushing past the guards who stepped aside. Reluctantly, and with a lot more attitude than was necessary, Ivy shoved the paper back into my hands and pressed a button opening the double doors. The security guards stepped away.

I turned back before the doors closed again. "I'll come out and let you know what's going on as soon as I know something," I said to Preppy's friends. King shot me an appreciative nod before I followed the nurse down the wide hall on the way to find Preppy.

My husband.

★ ★ ★

THE NURSE WALKED me through another set of doors and pointed me toward a curtain before stalking back off toward the waiting area, grumbling to herself along the way. Cautiously, I pulled the curtain aside and my breath caught in my throat when I saw Preppy lying there on the gurney with his head tilted back and his eyes closed. He was unconscious.

A doctor wearing glasses and a long white lab coat was hovering over Preppy, a needle up to the IV in the back of Preppy's hand. When the doctor realized I was there his eyes snapped up to mine and he pulled the needle from the IV and stood up straight, adjusting his coat.

"I'm his wife," I said before he could protest my presence. "What's going on with him?" I asked, standing by the gurney and taking Preppy's hand in mine in a very wifely move. I scanned him over but there weren't any obvious signs of injury. No bleeding or bruises. "What happened to him?"

The doctor tucked the full needle into the breast pocket of his shirt. "What is that?" I asked, pointing to where he'd just covered his pocket with his coat.

"Just a mild sedative," he replied, pushing his glasses back on his nose. That's when I noticed the cheesy smiley face tattoo on the back of his hand.

"He looks perfectly sedated to me," I said, looking at Preppy who's mouth was open, a deep snore rumbled from his mouth.

"That's why I decided not to give it to him," The doctor replied, jotting something down on his clipboard.

"Why sedate him at all? What exactly is going on here? Why is he here at all?"

"Your husband was found on the water tower about to commit suicide. It was called in by a concerned passer-by and the police called an ambulance who brought him here. Standard protocol for these types of things."

Suicide? The water tower?

"Who was the passer-by?" I asked. "I'd like to check with them. Talk to them about what it is they saw."

"You can't. It was an anonymous call." The doctor set the clipboard into a slot on the wall. "If you'll excuse me ma'am."

"No, I won't excuse you. There must be some mistake. The bystander is wrong. My husband wouldn't do that," I argued.

I knew Preppy's take on suicide. I knew that even in the worst of worst times he would never take his own life. I was as sure of that as I was about the earth being round and the sky being blue.

I want to be an old man with old rabbit dick dangling between my legs…

"Ma'am it doesn't matter if you think he would or wouldn't try to kill himself. We are checking him in to the psych ward for a full evaluation. We will know more in a few days and if everything checks out fine then he can go home in seventy-two hours."

"A few days?" I asked, dropping Preppy's hand and taking a step forward toward the doctor. "That's not going to happen," I argued. "No, he's coming home with me."

"Ma'am," the doctor said, looking annoyed. "The law…"

"Sir," I interrupted him. "The law states that he can only be be put on a psych hold for up to seventy-two hours if he is a threat to himself or others or if he's been arrested and the judge requests a determination of his mental state prior to arrangement." I knew this because I'd looked it up once after my father threatened me with the very same thing after heroin and I became fast friends. I just hoped the laws in Florida were similar to the ones in New York. "Is he being charged with anything?"

The doctor rubbed his temple. "Not to my knowledge."

"Okay, and I happen to know for a fact that my husband goes up to the water tower to relax from time to time and look down at the city he loves. If in fact someone called him in as a possible suicide attempt, then they were very mistaken."

"I'm sorry ma'am, there isn't anything I can do. He has to stay for a hold…"

I stood my ground. "Without proof that he was trying to harm himself, which you don't have since your witness was anonymous, then you have no grounds to hold him."

"She's right," said a male police officer who'd just stepped inside the curtained area. "It's the law. He's free to go."

"Fine," the doctor huffed. He pulled aside the curtain. "But if he ends up dead because you didn't think he was capable of killing himself, then it's on you." He pointed to the officer and shot him a disapproving sneer. "I assume you can take care of his cuff." The doctor then scribbled on a piece of paper and handed it to me. "Discharge papers," he mumbled as he left.

"Thank you," I said, turning to the officer when the doctor was out of earshot, "I really appreciate…"

"You know that's not really the law, right?" the officer asked. He uncured Preppy's wrist from the gurney. When he was done he crossed his arms and took a wide stance. He was huge in both presence and stature. The name on his badge read Wiggum. "Close though."

"I wasn't a hundred percent sure, but it was worth a try," I explained. "Preppy hates hospitals and I know for a fact he wouldn't do what they said he was trying to do." Suddenly something strange hit me. I looked up to the officer who didn't look like any of the cops I'd ever seen. Tattoos on his neck and hands. A chiseled jaw, a five o'clock shadow and dark shiny hair peaking out from under his police hat. "But if it isn't the law then why would you say it was? Why put your job at risk for someone you don't know?"

"Who said I didn't know him? Besides, I would be really fucking concerned about my job…" Officer Wiggum turned to me and whispered "If I were really a cop."

"If you're not a cop then who are you?" I asked as non police office Wiggum took a syringe out of a pencil case.

"Wait, what are you giving him?" I placed my hand in front of the IV and the needle pricked my skin as he was about to push on the plunger. He growled in annoyance. "I'm just someone who happened to be in the right place at the right time," he said, grabbing my wrist he tossed it out of his way. I licked the drop of blood from the back of my hand. "And calm your pretty face. I'm just giving him something that will wake him up a bit," he said, pushing on the plunger. "Whatever fucking horse tranquilizer they gave him when they arrested him was meant to keep him comatose for quite a while."

"Then how were they supposed to do an evaluation on him? That makes no sense."

"Something tells me they never planned on any sort of evaluation. Keep your eyes out around here. Shit's gone a little sideways. Don't trust anyone. Especially not the cops or even the doctors." He leaned over Preppy and gave each of his cheeks a couple of short slaps.

Preppy's eyelids fluttered. He moaned softly and the sound

shot straight to my heart. I was so focused on him waking up I didn't realize that the man in the officer's uniform had been staring at me. "What?" I asked, feeling uncomfortable under his dark glare.

"You must be Dre," he said, with no sort of emotion attached to the words.

"How did you know who I am?"

Finally he smiled although it was a small crooked smile. "I know everything," he stated. He stood and tipped his hat to me on the way out. He glanced at Preppy one final time. "I'll tell King and Bear he's going home. Don't leave his side and when he comes around tell Prep he owes me one. Again."

I nodded, "I will. Thank you." Before he could step away I realized something. "Wait! Who do I tell him he owes? Unless Wiggum is really your name?" I asked, pointing to his badge.

He shook his head and grinned.

"Name's Smoke."

CHAPTER SEVENTEEN

PREPPY

FOR A FEW moments before Dre realized I was awake I watched her. It had been so long since I'd seen her. Like REALLY seen her in the light, yet nothing and everything had changed. Her skin was clear and so were the whites of her eyes. She was a knock out as a strung out junkie but sober made me feel warm and tingly in every part of my body, even the one that had refused to work for weeks. Even though she's wearing short sleeves she makes the motion like she's pulling down on her sleeves to cover the scars on her arms which are now barely noticeable. It turned from a habit into a nervous quirk and it's fucking adorable.

Dre was talking with someone but I can't see who the fuck it was and I didn't care. I was still checking out Dre and not believing she was really there. She still bites the side of her thumb too and if you looked at her from the wrong angle it almost seems as if she's sucking on it which makes my useless dick twitch for the first time in eons.

Something about her having the same little quirks made me feel like I wasn't so out of the loop, although I knew when my inspection of Dre landed on the sparkling diamond on her left hand that out of the loop is a fucking understatement.

I suppress a laugh, still not wanting her to know I was conscious just yet when I realize that she's talking to Smoke and he's wearing a full police uniform. Fuck knows what that was about but what tickled me as funny was that his name badge said Wiggum. I wait until he's gone before saying, "Wiggum. Chief Wiggum is the police chief on the Simpsons."

"Good, you're awake. What were you doing on the water tower?" she asked, smoothing my hair from my face. I want to lean into her touch but instead I flinch, a little reflex I picked up courtesy of Chop and she withdrew her hand.

I flashed her the biggest smile I could, forgetting about my missing tooth. I must have looked a mess. "I…" I started, not really remembering why I was there in the first place, but when the memory hits and I recall the party. The ring. The backstreet boy I knocked out. THE KISS. I decide to go with the truth. Sort of. "I was looking for you."

"Were you trying to jump?" she asked, crossing her arms over her chest like she was both pissed and disappointed, but I couldn't linger on that because the motion pushed her tits up over the neckline of her shirt and suddenly I hated the inch or so of cotton hiding what I knew to be perfect pink nipples from me.

"No, but I might have been screaming a little. Okay, a lot. Someone must have called the cops about the lunatic on the water tower and they hauled me in thinking I was going to take the long leap to nowhere."

"But you weren't?" she asked, like she was making sure.

"No, Doc," I reassured her. She nodded and breathed out slowly, like she'd been holding her breath. "One of the officers must have gotten a little punchy," I said, feeling the knot on my forehead. "Fucker."

"King and Bear are in the waiting room. I'll go tell them you're ready to go home," she said standing up.

I grabbed her wrist and she sat back down. "No, Doc. I can't go back there. It's too." I stopped. "It's just too...everything."

"Where do you want to go?"

"With you," I said, pleading with my eyes. "I want to go with you."

"Preppy..." she started, looking down at her lap. "That's not a good idea."

"Because you're engaged?" I asked sounding more bitter than I intended. "'Cause married people can't get engaged, unless the rules have changed. Shit, everything else has changed. Wouldn't surprise me."

"No, because I'm not even going to be here long. I'm going home to help my dad the second the house sells and the realtor thinks that could be really soon. And I'm not—"

"Okay, so I'll only stay until it sells or until you go home."

Basically, I'll just be there for as long as you're there.

"Preppy," Dre said, sounding unconvinced. I was going to have to bring out the big guns.

"As your husband on record, don't I have to sign off on the sale?" I asked.

Doc straightened her spine, "Wait, what?"

"Even if it's on a technicality we're married, right? The house would be considered our marital property, therefore I'd have to sign off on the sale regardless of who's name the house is in."

"Fuck," Dre mouthed when she realized I was right. It was adorable when she swore.

"Sounds good. Maybe later. Right now I'm just looking for

you to say, 'yes, Preppy, I'd love for you to come and stay with me for a while.'"

"So...you're blackmailing me?" Doc asked.

I smiled. "Abso-fucking-lutley."

★ ★ ★

"THAT'S THE KID you're fucking?" Preppy asked, pointing to the screen saver on my phone. It was a picture of me and Brandon at my college graduation. I graduated in three years and had a big smile on my face. Brandon was holding up my diploma like it was a trophy.

For me, it kind of was.

"Excuse me?" I snatched my phone from his hand and pushing it into my back pocket. "He's not a kid," I argued.

"Oh yeah? Could have fooled me. He looks like Zach Effron or a backstreet boy circa 1997. I mean, come on, Doc, he doesn't even have any facial hair. I bet he hasn't sprouted any pubes yet either, looks a little too young for that. What kind of man doesn't have any fucking facial hair?"

I glared at the short beard on his face.

"I mean what kind of man *normally* doesn't have facial hair. My beardlessness was due to special circumstances."

"Such as?"

"Such as shit I don't want to fucking talk about," Preppy said. He then started to whistle as he opened the back slider and stepped out onto the deck.

"See, I told you this wasn't a good idea," Ray said walking in the door and setting down a garbage bag of what I assumed was Preppy's stuff onto the floor. "He won't talk to any of us. He won't tell us anything. Insists that everything's okay when people hauled in to the hospital for attempted suicides are not okay."

"I can hear you," Preppy said, coming back inside and grabbing the bag off the floor. "Thanks, kid."

"So what were you two arguing about?" Ray asked.

"Doc's fiancé Where is he by the way?"

"You mean, Brandon?" Ray asked.

"He means Brandon," I said with a smile. "And Brandon had to go home."

"Oh yeah? And why is that?" Preppy asked.

"Because, he missed his boyfriend," I said casually.

"Oh, okay, because his…wait. What?" Preppy asked.

Ray snorted. "Preppy, Brandon's gay." We both broke out into a fit of laughter while Preppy looked at us like we'd lost our damn minds.

"Hold the fucking phone. Brandon's gay?" Preppy asked like he hadn't heard it right the first time.

He leaned onto the counter on his elbows. "Fuck, I lost my hair, a portion of my fucking gut…and my gaydar?"

"Seems so," Ray said, planting a kiss on Preppy's cheek. She may not have noticed him flinch but I did. "I'll check up on you kids. Behave yourselves," she sang as she closed the front door behind her.

"Don't feel too bad. I missed the signs too when I first met him." I laughed at the memory. "I actually thought he was asking me out when I first met him until we actually went out and his boyfriend met us after the movie." I tried to ignore the thickness of the air around us. I tucked it away in the linen closet, trying to pretend like his every word didn't make me feel something I didn't want to feel. Relief. Lust. LOVE. "So back to your earlier question. The kind of man who likes a clean look. That's who doesn't have facial hair."

"Oh yeah?" he asked, taking a step forward, crowding me in, staring down into my eyes with an intensity that had me biting down hard on my lower lip. "Do YOU like a clean look, Doc? Or do you like it dirty. Beards. Tattoos…scars."

Yes, I like it dirty. So dirty.

I was stunned into silence. His proximity was fucking with my brain and I was afraid that at any second I was going to blurt out something that would dig me a deeper hole than I'd already dug for myself. I opened my mouth to answer, but I couldn't get the words out. Not like I needed to. Preppy answered for me. "If I remember correctly, you like it dirty. *Real* fucking dirty."

He took another step toward me. "Remember that first time? In the field? By the train tracks? Remember how I pulled your hair while I fucked you from behind and stretched you open? Remember how it felt to have me moving inside of you? How it felt when you came and screamed in my fucking ear? I do. I remember. Thought of that scream every fucking day since. It was deafening." He chuckled and pressed his teeth against his bottom lip. He groaned, the sound shooting straight to my pussy. "I can still fucking hear it now."

So can I.

The hair on the back of my neck stood on end. "What are you doing?" I asked, trying to step out from under him, but he moved his arms and pressed his hands against the wall, caging me in. The warmth of his chest radiated onto mine and I tried to look anywhere but into his eyes, afraid of what I might see but there wasn't anywhere else to look. Especially when his face moved closer to mine.

He pressed his knee between my thighs, parting my legs. "Me?" he asked, with mock innocence. "I'm just reminiscing with an old friend."

"This doesn't feel like just reminiscing," I panted.

He stared deeply into my eyes. "No, not YET it doesn't." He grinned. "But it fucking will. Soon."

"I…I can't," I stammered. I pulled my face from his hand but he turned me back by my chin.

"Oh Doc, you remember how much I love it when you tell me no." He lowerd himself until his lips were a hair away from mine. My nipples peaked at the anticipation of feeling his lips against mine.

Maybe, just this once. I lied to myself. One more time just to remember how he felt when we…

A car door slammed in the driveway, throwing a bucket of cold water on the sizzling heat between us.

Preppy looked up and I jumped under his arm and away from him, again busying myself with folding towels. I cleared my throat and adjusted my shirt, trying to hide my hardened nipples underneath my thin tank top. "That would be the realtor," I said, as casually as possible.

"Great," Preppy said, blowing out a breath.

"And when he leaves we need to talk," I said, trying not to sound affected by him.

"About what?" Preppy asked. The doorbell rang.

I adjusted my hair and right before I opened the door to let in the realtor and his clients I turned back to Preppy and swallowed hard.

"Our divorce."

DRE

We never did have a conversation about a divorce although we needed to have it at some point. Or maybe an annulment instead, but I was pretty sure if there were time restrictions on those type of things that we'd long surpassed it. We didn't talk about what happened to him either.

Or much of anything else for that matter.

It had been a little over a week since Preppy moved in. He rarely came out of Mirna's old room and I noticed when he did it was only at night. If he ever was up and about during the day the first thing he would do was shut the blinds and put his sunglasses on. I knew he was having trouble with light and I saw at the party what happened to him when the volume of life around him got too loud.

There were flashes of the old Preppy from time to time. A snide remark. Innuendo about my short skirts. The burning glare of desire in his sad eyes that made my knees weak and my heart want to burst inside my chest.

Several times a night he'd scream through his nightmares and when I tried to go in to help him I couldn't. The door was always locked. I'd sit in the hallway with my back on the other side of the door and listen to him battle whatever demons he fought off in his dreams until the screams subsided.

When I couldn't sleep I'd fire up my laptop and research conditions of people who'd gone through traumatic situations. Counseling and medication were the two recommendations although Preppy would NEVER agree to counseling and self medicating was more his thing.

I sighed and bookmarked the page, clicking over to the Logan's Beach realty site to see if anything else had recently sold in the area and I was surprised that several homes in need of more repair and priced much higher had recently sold. I made a note to call East if there was something wrong with our listing, especially since the potential buyers the realtor showed the house to never came back with an offer and there hadn't been a single interested buyer since then. Although part of me was relieved it hadn't sold yet, part of me was frantic to make it happen. With the auction date approaching time was running out for my dad. I had to think of another creative way to either sell the house or make a substantial amount of money and FAST.

"Dad?" I asked when my phone rang. "Dad is everything okay? It's late."

"Everything's fine here. I was just checking to make sure everything is okay there. Brandon told me what happened with that boy and I was concerned that..." He paused and I heard his guilt dripping into the phone.

"You wanted to know if I was using again."

"Yes," my dad answered honestly.

"No, dad. I'm not. I haven't thought about it," I said, and with that statement I was proud. "Although I had two glasses of wine with a friend the other night and guess what happened..." I said.

"What?"

"Absolutely nothing," I whispered. "Except maybe a lot of laughter and me falling asleep before eight pm."

My dad laughed softly. "I'm so proud of you, Andrea."

I stood up and walked out into the backyard. The cool night air felt like heaven against my damp skin. After I slid the door shut I turned around and jumped back against the door, dropping my phone.

"Hello?" I heard my dad saying. I leaned down and picked up the phone. "Hey dad. Everything is fine, but I have to go. I'll call you back in the morning." I clicked the phone shut and slowly descended the steps. My eyes focused on Preppy who was sitting in the backyard under the light of the moon with his face tilted up toward the sky, moaning and rocking from side to side as if he were in pain.

Naked.

Very VERY naked.

The brutal red and white scars slashing through his once beautiful tattoos made me want to run my hands over them as if I could heal him. I wanted to weep for him and kill the fucker who did this to him.

I stepped around him and crouched down so we were at eye level. His eyes shot open. His bloodshot and unfocused gaze met mine.

"Help me."

"How do you want me to help you?" I whispered. I didn't know what kind of episode he was having. Fuck, I didn't even know if he was awake so I didn't want to scare him by talking too loud.

He reached out and pushed the string of my tank top off my shoulder. His touch made my body shudder. He pushed off the other strap and then tugged at the hem of my shirt. "Please," he begged softly, but there was nothing sexual about what he was asking. There was no desire in his eyes. Only pain.

I slowly undressed, pulling down my panties and stepping

out of them before kneeling down before him. "Come here," he whispered, tugging me by the shoulders until I was straddling him. He was partially hard, just feeling him against me made me want to throw caution to the wind and put him inside of my body but this wasn't about me.

I wasn't even really sure what it was really about but whatever it was, he needed it so I was going to do my best to give it to him.

He wrapped his arms around my waist and pressed his head against my naked chest. He breathed in and out slowly like he was trying to steady himself and then I realized he was trying not to cry. A few moments later his shoulders shook.

"Let go," I whispered, holding him tighter against me. "Let it all go,"

Preppy's shoulders shook harder and I felt his warm tears against my skin. I felt my own tears start and once they did I couldn't stop them.

So there we sat. In the backyard. Naked. Wrapped in each other's arms until the sun came up.

I woke up in the grass, covered by a blanket.

Preppy was gone.

I trudged back up to the house and thought back to when I first met Preppy. I was vulnerable. Weak. Everyone in my life had tried to tip-toe around me while they worked their asses off to save me.

Not Preppy.

It pained me that I had to leave Logan's Beach when the house sold. It broke my heart that Preppy and I could never have a shot at anything real, not once he learned about the secret I was keeping from him. But I smiled to myself anyway, because when I was weak Preppy saved me by giving me his strength.

CHAPTER EIGHTEEN

PREPPY

"DID WE FUCK?" I asked Dre who dropped a fork. I knew we didn't but I loved getting a reaction out of her. "I mean I don't think we did. But I woke up naked on the porch. Wasn't the first time I've slept outside, but I don't remember actually going out there."

"No we didn't fuck," Dre said. My dick twitched when she said FUCK and I made a note to make her swear more at me from now on because it was the first sign that my cock wasn't useless after all. "I think you were sleepwalking." She was irritated which made me believe that me naked on the porch was more than a simple case of sleepwalking.

"You have to be nice to me, Doc," I said, scraping a chair against the tile as I pulled it out from the table. I pulled the other one out as well. I sat on one, propping my legs up on the other, crossing my feet at the ankles. I opened her laptop and pulled up the page she had bookmarked and pointed to it. "I have post pardum depression."

Dre snorted through a burst of laughter, wrinkling her nose. I'm instantly hit with an ache to my balls but it's not an ache I mind. Not at all. Actually it's the first even remotely pleasurable sensation in that region of my body I'd had since I came back from the brink. "Um…Preppy?" she asked, not waiting for me to answer. "Postpartum depression is what happens to some women after…after having babies. What I think you mean is something called post traumatic stress disorder."

I waved her off. "Listen just because I call you Doc doesn't mean you're a medical expert," I said, eliciting another small burst of laughter as she rolled and uncovered a ball of dough that had been rising in a bowl on the counter. "Besides, it doesn't matter what the fuck it's called, what matters is that I have it, so what I'm saying is that I'll need to be taken care of. WELL taken care of. Mmmmmmkay?" I asked and when she flashed me a 'what the fuck ever' look I stuck out my lower lip in an exaggerated and what I could only imagine was a very pathetic looking pout.

"Oh yeah? Is that so?" Dre asked, turning around with one hand on her jutted out hip, one perfectly arched eyebrow craning upward toward her hairline, and her deep red fuckable lips quirked to the side. "And what kind of HELP is it that you're in so much desperate need of?"

I opened my mouth to say my usual something sarcastic but at the last second I cleared my throat and even I didn't expect what poured from my lips. My voice was much lower and raspier than a moment before. An almost-whisper. "All of it. I need all of the help." There was no trace of any kind of humor in my words. What was I even trying to tell her?

Dre seemed to be mulling over what I'd just said. Her lips flattening into a straight line. She looked over the sink through the window into the neglected back yard. The sun shifted out from behind a cloud and her face brightened instantly, illuminated by the early morning rays. She paused there for what seemed like a motherfucking eternity, closing her eyes and soaking up the warm light.

The clock above the stove ticked louder and louder as it announced each passing second until it turned into tick-ticking insanity pounding within my ear drums. TICK-TOCK TICK-TOCK.

Finally, Dre broke through my impatience when she turned to me again and wiped her flowery hands on her apron. Her lips turned upward in a bright white, full-toothed smile that covered her entire face. My heart sped up like it had been hit with electric paddles, so much so it skipped a beat and I coughed into the crook of my elbow. "Okay, then."

"Okay then…what?" I asked, casually looking down at my hands and turning them over as if I was inspecting my own tattoos.

"Okay then if you need help, I'll give it to you." She paused and I hadn't realized she'd crossed the kitchen until I looked up from my hands and found her standing over me, so close her knee was pressed against my thigh. I craned my neck to look up at her face. "But my help is conditional."

"What kind of conditions?" I asked, she stepped away.

"Why are you pushing me away, Doc?" I asked, hating the feeling of space between us.

She turned suddenly, her face serious. "Because you hurt me! Because you fucking destroyed me! Because when you pushed me away last time I might as well have died with you. And I went to rehab and school and there were a million times when I wanted to call you and talk to you and tell you about my day and I couldn't because you decided that we shouldn't be together.

YOU. Not us, YOU. Then you fucking died on me and I fucking hated you for it. All of it!"

"You're mad at me because…I died?"

"Yes, and because you never knew the truth. There are so many things you need to know that I never told you."

"So tell me, Doc," I said. She shook her head.

"Please, everyone else spares me from the truth because they're afraid I'll fall apart. That's what's driving me more crazy than any of the other shit. Just tell me the fucking truth!"

"You might hate me."

"I might."

"Okay," she agreed, with a small nod. She straightened her spine. "Then come on," she said, checking the clock on the stove. "We have time to make it."

"Where are we going?" I asked, confused why this conversation needed a field trip.

"To the truth."

DRE

"So THAT'S HOW this all works?" Preppy asked, pointing to the man at the podium. "You just get up there and tell a shit load of strangers about all your fuck ups?"

My lips curved up into a smile at Preppy's choice of wording. "Pretty much, it's supposed to unburden the soul and remind you that you're not alone. You should try it sometime. It's very freeing." I scrunched my nose in thought. "Well, not right away, but eventually it feels very freeing," I amended. "Sometimes."

"Yeah, I get all that, but who the fuck has that much time?"

I swatted him with the pamphlet they'd given me on the way in which is what I assume they give out at most of the NA meetings. A schedule of meetings and a list of people you can call if you feel like using again.

"Why are you all the way back here?" Preppy asked in a loud whisper, scooting closer to me in the pew. "Isn't the meeting in the front where all those other people are?"

"I just…don't feel like I need to be up there right now," I explained, although not really explaining anything at all.

"I don't get it," Preppy said, forgetting to whisper. Several heads turned around to see where the commotion was coming from and I flashed them an apologetic smile although I really wasn't sorry. Preppy wasn't a conformist. Being quiet, especially in a setting like a church was a huge undertaking for him. I was actually kind of impressed he wasn't doing cartwheels up and down the isles. "I don't always sit in the back. It just depends on…on how I'm doing."

"I still don't get it, Doc, use small words if you have to but explain it to me."

"Okay, so like right now I'm sitting in the back pew by the door, just listening. It's like being back here makes me feel like I'm straddling this invisible line separating the meeting going on up there and the outside world, which is how I feel most of the time. Like I don't quite belong up there, but I know I need to be here in some way."

"What about on other days?" Preppy asked, seeming genuinely interested in what I was about to say.

"There are some days that are a little harder," I admitted. "Days when I'm up there with the others, participating, telling my story, because I feel like the outside world doesn't get it and I need to be up there with people who do."

"How long has it been since you've been up there?" Preppy asked, just as Steve, the meeting leader, called out my name.

"Andrea, are you ready?" Steve asked, gesturing to the empty `podium with a smile.

I nodded to Steve and stood. "I'll be up there in about three seconds." My heart hammered in my chest as I shuffled sideways out of the pew. "I'll understand if you want to leave before I'm done," I added, looking him over one last time.

He wanted the truth and I was about to give it to him in a big way.

The BIGGEST way.

"I'm not going anywhere," he reassured me, although there was no way he knew what exactly he was agreeing to. I made my way to the front of the church where the small wooden podium was positioned directly in front of the pews in the center of the aisle. I looked over the crowd of a dozen or so other men and women, a few teenagers in the crowd and I took a deep breath.

Preppy flashed me one last reassuring smile from the back pew and I hoped it wouldn't be the last.

"My name is Andrea," I started, my voice shaky. "But everyone calls me Dre. I'm an addict. Heroin was my weapon of choice if you're interested in knowing." I looked over the crowed. "And I've been sober for a few years now."

My introduction was met with several "Hi' Dre's" from the crowd and a few claps of encouragement. "You know, I've been to a thousand of these meetings. I've introduced myself to hundreds of others just this same way." I shook my head and cleared my throat. "For some reason stupid reason I keep expecting this to get easier." The crowd laughed. "But telling my story never does."

Steve chimed in from the front row, "It may never get easier, but it's a good reminder of why you are here and why you can never go back."

There were more words of encouragement murmured from the small crowd, but it wasn't their reaction that had me holding onto the edges of the podium for support. I cast one last glance to Preppy in the back row. He was partially hidden in the shadows so I couldn't make out his expression and in that moment I was grateful for it.

I continued. "I've been sober now for several years. I've lost people. I guess that's how this all started. I lost my step-sister and I blamed myself. Her boyfriend blamed me too, and we fell into our addictions together. He became violent. He…he hurt me. He RAPED me. I told myself I deserved it. In the end, I lost him too." I took a deep breath and looked down at the podium.

"I almost killed myself one night. I almost jumped off of the water tower right here in Logan's Beach. But I was saved by someone. I wouldn't call him a guardian angel exactly. More like a devil with good timing.

"After a bunch of other stuff that I won't bore you with, I sobered up and my dad took me back and I checked into rehab.

"One night, not long after I'd gotten there, I realized how fucking tired I was. Not like sleep tired, but tired of hurting. Because just when I thought my heart couldn't break anymore it kept shattering over and over again and after a while, just when I thought I was going to be okay...I couldn't take it anymore.

"And as an addict, I only knew of one way I could make it all go away.

"I don't even remember how I managed to escape the rehab facility, or what door or window I snuck out of. All I know is that night, less than an hour after thinking about using again, I was sitting on the dirty floor of some dealers drug den holding a lighter in one hand and a spoon in the other."

I paused. My chest tightened. I fought back the tears that threatened every single time I was about to start on the next part. The most important part. The tears won and by the time I started speaking they were falling in warm streams down my cheeks.

"That night everything changed in a flash of a second. Before I could tie off my arm, my gut twisted. I thought it could've been the guilt of what I was about to do. And I think it could have been a part of it, but when it passed I tied off my arm and just as I lifted the needle to prick my skin a pain tore through my stomach and I blacked out.

"I woke up in the hospital thinking that I'd overdosed. My dad was there and he told me I didn't have any drugs in my system. He had tears in his eyes and when I asked him what was wrong," my voice cracked. "He told me he wanted to be the one to tell me himself that I..." I took a deep breath to compose myself. "Sorry. He wanted to be the one to tell me the news that I'd lost a baby. My baby," I said, a sob escaping my lips. "A baby I didn't even know I was carrying for fifteen weeks. A little girl.

"I loved her the second he told me about her and I grieved her as hard as any mother can grieve for the loss of a child. When the guilt came again, the overwhelming maddening guilt, it crashed into me a thousand times worse than it ever had before and I realized that she was never fated to make it in this life.

"If it weren't for those pains I would have used and I know in my heart that she wouldn't of made it if I had. Or possibly me as well. That sweet unborn baby, who never stood a chance at taking her first breath, stopped me from making the biggest mistake of my life.

"She saved my life.

"After I got out of the hospital I checked back into rehab and I never touched a needle again. And every time I feel myself sliding down into the abyss I find comfort in thinking about her. In a way I like to think that talking about her gives her a new kind of life, because although it was short, it had so much meaning. SHE had meaning.

"I was slipping. I wasn't strong enough to save myself, But it turns out that she was strong enough for the both of us. So now it's my job to be strong for her," I scanned the crowd and my eyes fell on the motionless shadow in the back row. "And I have no intentions of ever letting her down."

I LEFT RIGHT after my speech, not waiting until the end. I walked down the aisle to find the last row empty. Pain welled in my chest as I told myself that it was expected. There would be no reason for him to stick around after what I'd just said. I knew he'd be angry, I knew he'd hate me for what I'd done and he had every right to. But he had a right to know and although I was crushed he wasn't there, a big part of me was glad he finally knew about his daughter.

I pushed open the double doors that lead to the front room of the church from the chapel and was about to exit through the front when a voice stopped me. "She was mine?"

I turned to find Preppy standing against the wall in the corner, his expression unreadable. "I thought you left."

"She was mine?" he repeated.

I nodded.

"Fuck you," he spat. "Why didn't you come tell me? Why…" he stopped, pushed off the wall and came to stand in front of me. His eyes rimmed in red as they searched mine for answers.

"After how we left things I didn't think you'd really care and even if you would care what would be the point? It was too late, there wasn't anything that could be done."

"I would've cared," he argued. "And I could've been there for you."

"I wouldn't have known that," I responded, biting my bottom lip and I could tell from the shift in his expression that he understood.

"You…" he started, his eyebrows furrowed. He glanced down to my stomach in confusion and reached out, placing his flattened palm over the fabric of my dress then bunching the fabric in his hands. I felt the warmth of his hand through the material of my dress as if he were touching bare skin. "You were carrying my baby," his voice almost a whisper.

Although it wasn't a question, I nodded, sniffling and shuffling my feet as he continued to stare at me as if he were seeing me for the first time.

"You had to go through that all alone," he said. "My baby…"

"I'm so sorry," I said, filling the awkward silence. "My body was still recovering and too weak to carry her and I'm so…"

"Stop," Preppy said, holding up a hand.

"But…"

"Stop!" he said. "God damnit, Doc! You should have told

me. I would've been there for you. I would have come running if I knew you'd just lost our baby. You shouldn't have been alone for that."

"I'm just so so…"

My apology was cut short when Preppy descended on me, crushing his lips against mine. I squealed as a surprising bolt of confusion and desire pulsed through my entire body as his kiss grew deeper and more desperate. He lifted me off my feet and swung me around, pushing my back against the wall next to a door marked OFFICE. I opened my mouth to him and when our tongues tangled together he groaned and used his knee to spread my legs further apart. My dress rode up my thighs, one less layer between us as his hands met my bare ass.

A thin strip of wet cotton was all that was left to cover me.

Preppy rocked against me, groaning. I gasped into his mouth when I felt his hard cock, huge and ready, against my core. "I thought," I started, searching his face. The chords in his neck were tight. His face was flushed.

Preppy chuckled and spoke against my lips. "I thought too, Doc. I guess my cock was just waiting for the right place and time."

"A church during an NA meeting?" I asked with a smile, panting as my body responded to his every touch. He rocked against me again, harder this time. My insides clenched, needing him to fill me, wanting him deep inside of me.

"If my cock wants to fuck you in a church then who the fuck am I to argue?" Preppy asked before pressing his lips back to mine and continuing the agony of the most passion filled kiss I'd ever experienced in my life. "I'll take it as a sign from God that I should fuck you right here and now."

"What?" I asked breathlessly, as Preppy dipped one hand between us pushing my panties aside. The second his fingers connected with my delicate flesh I bucked off the wall and Preppy grabbed me tighter by the waist, pulling me in closer, locking me to him.

"Shhhh, gonna fuck you, Doc. Gonna make you come so hard you're gonna drip down my fucking cock," he said, his voice low and raw as he circled my aching clit and I writhed for more.

"Is that what's happening? We're fucking?" I asked. "Because there is a room full of people in there that will be coming out of those doors in about ten minutes or so."

He stared deep into my eyes. "Doc, I've waited way too long for this. I don't care that it's in a church. I don't care if we have an audience gathered around us. I don't care if the cops show up and try to drag us away because I won't let them. All I care about is this and us. Right now. Right fucking now," he groaned inserting a finger inside me. "Holy fucking shit, Doc. You're tighter than I remember. Holy fucking shit." Preppy looked around and then back to me. "Here," he said, reaching for the door handle marked office and carrying me inside the small room. "But only because I know once I get inside that tight fucking pussy that I won't want to come out for a while."

My insides screamed for his words to be reality and I was embarrassingly wet, dripping down my inner thighs.

Inside the room was small. A few computers lined one of the walls with a desk in the middle and a small couch on the other side. At one of the computers, sitting in the dark, was a portly guy around his early thirties with a shaved head. When we barged into the room he stood up abruptly, knocking over a chair as Preppy set me down but didn't let me get too far, he held me close to his side. "Get out," Preppy instructed the man.

"Hey! Hey you guys can't be in here," he said, pulling up his dress slacks which were already well above his bellybutton and fumbling to close his zipper.

"Get out now or before the pastor finds out that his assistant pastor was in here looking at porn during church hours," Preppy warned, nodding to where a naked busty blonde was laying spread eagle on the screen of the computer the man had just been sitting at.

"Preppy? Is that you?" The man said, adjusting his glasses and taking a step closer. "You know; I'd heard that you were back but I didn't..."

"Out now. We'll catch up later," Preppy asked with a certain amount of pleading in his demand.

"Oh yeah, of course, man," he said, gathering up some papers from the desk. He tossed Preppy set of keys on his way out the door. "Lock up and put the key in the donation bin outside the door. Good to see you Preppy," he called back, sounding both cheerful and just a little bit afraid as the door clicked shut.

Preppy checked to make sure the door was shut but there was no lock to turn which explains why the assistant minister hadn't locked it either.

Preppy wasted no time bringing my mouth back to his. He reached under my dress and pulled down my panties which I stepped out of. He backed me deeper into the room as I fumbled for his belt, grabbing him in my hand I gave his hot flesh a squeeze and his head fell back against the wall. His eyes closed. I squeezed again and he pushed my hand away, letting his pants drop to the floor. I went down to my knees, wanting to taste what was dripping down the tip of his glorious cock when he grabbed me by the elbows and kept me upright. “I want your mouth, Doc. I want all of you. But it’s been too fucking long and I just need to be inside of you. Right fucking now.”

“I just wanted to taste you,” I admitted, biting my bottom lip.

“Agh, don’t say shit like that. I want to last more than a minute,” he said, pulling me against him and kissing me until we were both groaning and writhing against one another. His fingers found my wetness and parted my folds, first one, then another fingers slowly entered me and I felt like as if I were going to combust. Heat, pleasure, sparks, and so much more pinged around in my body, turning every pleasure sense I had on high alert. I was alive with anticipation, a need arose inside me so fierce Preppy had be begging him with each stroke of his fingers.

“Preppy,” I begged, needing more.

Hearing the desperation in my voice and feeling it in my humming body he picked me up and pushed me against the arm of the couch, he pushed open my thighs, fisted his cock and lined himself up with my opening he pushed inside, just a half an inch and then he paused. I looked up to find him staring at me. “I can’t believe this is really happening. It’s you,” he said, repeating the words from the first time we saw each other again.

“It’s me,” I breathed, holding onto the sides of his face as he thrust the rest of the way inside of me. I cried out, not knowing who was around and not caring who heard. The fullness was shredding me open on the inside in the most delicious way. Pain only led to pleasure, especially when Preppy spoke, his words fanning the flames of the fire that was already burning volcano hot. “Fuck, Doc. You’re so fucking tight. Holy shit. Your fucking pussy is so tight it almost hurts. How is this possible…ahhhhh,” he cried out, closing his eyes tight. "You feel so fucking good. Better than I remember. Fucking perfect."

"No one, since you," I admitted, the pleasure and emotions crashing into me so hard tears again dripped from the corners of my eyes as I struggled to maintain a hold on it all.

His eyes shot open and met mine and he smiled. His eyes half hooded, when our eyes met. He reached down and lifted my dress up above my breasts. and leaned over me, pushing me back further onto the couch, bringing my knees up against his chest as he gave me every inch of his big cock, pushing inside of me in long hard strokes. The way he pulled out brushed my tender bundle of nerves just inside my pussy and sent sparks up my spine.

Over and over again the sparks ignited until my entire body was on fire, an inferno of need ready to combust. Preppy picked up his speed. "You're so fucking close. I feel it. Kiss me. Kiss me when you fucking come."

Our lips met and I closed my eyes on instinct, lost in sensation. "Open your eyes," he demanded. "Kiss me and look at me when you come. I want you to see me," he said. Three more thrusts, I lifted up my hips as much as I could in my position to take as much of him as I could. With my eyes open and my lips on his, the fire burned out of control, shooting down my spine, my entire body contracted and spasmed in one endless burst of pleasure that had me screaming into Preppy's mouth. I was still riding my orgasm by writhing on his cock when he stilled and our lips separated as he growled through his own release, hot streams spilled inside of me, his cock pulsing for what seemed like minutes. Even after he pulled himself from me a minute later spurts of white were still dripping from the tip, falling onto my clit.

"Holy fucking shit," Preppy said, trying to catch his breath.

I laid there, at an awkward angle on the side of the couch, staring at a cross painted on the low ceiling of the office. My limbs jello as I tried to remember how to breathe or even sit up.

Or even my own fucking name.

"Yeah," I agreed. "I mean, it was okay."

Preppy chuckled and fell on top of me, clutching my face in his hands. "Hey, Doc?" he asked, searching my eyes. His laugh quieted and his smile fell.

My stomach flipped. "Yeah?"

"This time…I'm gonna keep you."

"Don't make promises you can't keep," I said.

He looked into my eyes and stroked my cheek. "I'm gonna try my fucking hardest to keep you."

CHAPTER NINETEEN

PREPPY

WE WERE STILL in bed when I turned to Doc. Her hair was a mess, sticking out a million ways from her head. Her red lipstick was smeared all over her cheeks.

She was fucking gorgeous. I pulled her leg so her thigh was resting over mine.

"What did you do before, you know, to de-stress? For fun?" Doc asked, twirling a shiny lock of her hair between her fingers. Of course the first thing that came to my mind was fucking, although fucking anyone other than her was more like a chore. A struggle in trying not to hurt anyone while trying to take some sort of pleasure out of the situation. Until Dre, I'd failed at it. I'd failed a LOT. Still, I must have had that dirty look in my eye. "Other than that," she said, nudging my shoulder. "What's something you haven't done in a while? Something we can do together? Right now."

A smile crept onto my face and I smiled at my girl like a fool as one thing came to mind that always made me feel better once I'd done it. "There is ONE thing..." My smile grew even bigger. "Tell me, Doc." I leaned in close, "How do you feel about misdemeanors?"

"They have their uses."

"Come on. I'll show you how much fun those uses can be."

Twenty minutes later we were standing in front of the Stop-N-shop in the shadows where the one overhead light in the parking light couldn't reach. We had a full view of the heavily pimpled man-child working the counter, but there was no way he could see us.

"On the count of three," I said, "One..."

"Wait, why are we doing this again?" Dre asked with a giggle that made my balls tighten.

"Because revenge is sweet and bullying is wrong, don't you read the papers? These people need to be taught a lesson for future generations."

"He bullied you?" she asked, sounding as if he'd also kicked her puppy.

"Yep, used to kick my ass all the time in grade school. You know, I won though, but it was still super annoying."

"That fucker!"

"Exactly. So are we doing this or what, Doc? If you're in it's pick up that pretty skirt and grab your balls. Are you in or are you out?"

She didn't hesitate. "Oh, I'm in alright." Dre raised her arm in launch position and tipped her chin to me. "Ready!"

I started the countdown. "One... Two... Three!" On three we both threw as hard as we can, not stopping until the two dozen eggs in the carton were all gone and smashed against the window. "It's fucking beautiful," Dre said, admiring the smears and drips of liquid yolk sliding down the glass, the lights from inside the store gave what we did a backlit effect, making it look as if the window was glowing.

"We should probably run," I suggested, hearing the ding of the front door and the stomp of angry steps across the pavement.

"Sure, where do you want to go now…"

"No, we should run!" I yelled, grabbing her arm and dragging her with me until she realized that Tyler was right behind us as well as blue and red lights of a patrol car that had just skid into the parking lot.

"Shit!" Dre squealed sounding more delighted than one should be when the possibility being cuffed in the back of a squad car by the end of the night was pretty fucking high.

"This way," I said, leading her over the chain link fence in the back of the store and then down the path that twisted through a wooded area and ended up across the road from my house. We darted over dead plants and tree roots, my memory of the path I used to know so well the only thing guiding us forward on the dark path. Dre squealed again when we heard the sound of the fence rattling. A mini tunnel of brightness darted from side to side ahead of us, courtesy of a strong ass cop flashlight.

"Stop, you're under arrest!" ordered the officer chasing us.

"If we keep going this way he's going to catch up to us. We need a better plan," Dre pointed out.

She was right. I wasn't the only one who knew the path, but suddenly, like an idea bulb growing bright, a light came into view in the distance from a house that definitely didn't exist last time I was in those woods. Laughter and soft rock music filled the air. A clink of glasses. A splashing of water. The smell of meat on a grill. It seemed as if someone was having a barbecue, and those someones were about to have two new best friends.

"Come on," I said, hopping over the little white picket fence lining the backyard. As we ran toward the back of the house

I realized it wasn't a bar-b-que as much as a couple, two men sitting in a small hot tub on their back deck, drinking red wine while a closed grill smoked just a few feet away. The outdoor table was set for four, complete with plates and glasses, as if they were expecting more company.

"What the hell are you…" Dre started to ask as I stripped off my clothes.

"Take off your clothes," I told her. "Now."

"Who the hell are you?" the younger man of the two asked, standing up in the water to reveal the smallest speedos no man should ever be subjected to seeing in his lifetime. The other man, a silver haired older gentleman, looked mildly amused and very VERY high. They must have smoked earlier because although the source of it wasn't laying around, the light smell of weed still lingered in the air.

"We, gentleman, are your company for the night," I announced, "And we've been here all day," I added, glancing back into the woods, the beam of the light was growing closer. "I'm Samuel and this is my wife Dre." Dre gave them a small wave as she continued to undress. She added one of her famous huge red lipped smiles too although I was sure it wasn't as effective on them as it always seemed to be on me.

I grabbed the bottle of wine from the ledge on the side of the tub and poured it into the two empty glasses lining the place settings. Dre kicked off her shoes until she was only in her underwear and bra. She picked up her clothes and mine and tossed them into the open kitchen window. The men watched her with confused expressions on their faces. The man who was standing slowly sank back down into the bubbling water. "And if you play along with what's about to happen, I'll give you a six-month supply of the best weed you can get your hands on in all of Logan's Beach."

The older man seemed to be thinking over my offer although I'd wished he'd think it over faster. MUCH FASTER. "That would be good because the stuff I bought today across the bridge was…how you say… shit," he said with a very heavy Spanish accent. I stepped into the hot tub in only my boxers, my legs having no choice but to brush against speedo-man in the small tub. I handed Dre her glass of wine and helped her into the tub next to me. I grabbed a handful of water and wet my hair before wrapping my arm around Dre's shoulders and pulling her close to my side.

"I'm Fred and that sexy gentleman is Meryl," Fred announced before playfully swatting Meryl on the shoulder. "And you said we should have built in Miami because there is no excitement in Logan's Beach." He held his glass up in our direction, and then gasped with whispered delight when the officer hopped the back fence and started heading our way. "How much more excitement do you need?" he said, behind his hand as if the officer could read lips in the dark.

By the time the officer got to us, out of breath with leaves and twigs stuck all over his dark blue uniform, the four of us were in full fake conversation, laughing and clinking our glasses together like old friends.

"Is this the friend you said was joining us?" Dre asked, she turned to the officer. "Did you bring more wine?" She downed her glass. "'Cause this is goooood stuff."

"You always did have a taste for the expensive," Fred teased, sounding like a natural born actor. "What can we do for you officer…Beaman?" he asked with a flirty tone, cocking his head to the side to read his badge.

"You two," Beaman said, pointing from me to Dre. "Out of there right now. You're under arrest for vandalism, evading an officer of the law…"

"I think you're mistaken, Sir," I said. "You've got the wrong people. We've been here for hours with our friends having a good time. We did hear some rustling in the brush though, so you might want to check the woods." I smiled and took a sip of my wine which was actually pretty fucking good considering I didn't know shit about wine.

"Don't make me add more charges to the list," the officer warned, placing his hand on his gun and playfully tapping his fingers over the strapped buttoned over the holster. "Like failure to cooperate with an investigation, and…"

"Wait just a second officer. These are our guests in our home and they've been here all night like they said. Now move on and keep searching for who you're mistaking them for," Fred argued.

Beaman shook his head and didn't take his eyes from me as he said, "I'm not mistaking anything, sir. Now you two get the fuck out of there and come with me or I'll…" he flicked the strap on his holster open.

This single move pissed me off to the point that my vision blurred with anger. Normally, as if anything were ever fucking normal, this little show of power would be the trigger setting me off into a rage that ended up with me calling Smoke for a body cleanup. But I didn't want to put Dre in any sort of danger. I couldn't.

It was only a misdemeanor. What the hell.

Score:

Preppy: 78,903,948,098

Law: 1

I guess I could go with him this once.

I was about to set my wine glass down and do as he said when Meryl stood up, the water beaded on his chest and slid down over his curly grey chest hair, landing in a puddle over his pot belly which hid whatever speedo he was wearing.

God I hoped he was wearing a speedo.

"Let me ask you a little something, did you see these two commit the crime you are accusing them of?" Meryl asked, sternly, taking a very professional stance as if he weren't mostly naked.

Or possibly naked.

Shit, he was most definitely naked.

The officer sighed in frustration. "No, but we saw them running and got a call…"

"Running isn't illegal," he argued. "If it were them that is. Which it most certainly was not."

Officer Beaman opened his mouth to protest but Meryl cut him off. "Furthermore officer," Meryl stressed the word OFFICER, "this is private property, where I am entertaining guests, and you, having not witnessed whatever the crime is in question, have no legal right to be on my property. If you feel the need to come back or think you have valid legal reason to do so, you are welcome to come back with a warrant, or else my office will be dealing with you and believe me that they will rain down the wraith of an angry old man six months from retirement, trying to enjoy his vacation, the likes of which you have NEVER seen!" Meryl reached toward the table, plucked his wallet from his jeans and handed the officer a card.

I was downright shocked when Officer Beamans eyes went wide and he tipped his hat to Meryl, offering his apologies. "So sorry to have disturbed your party, sir."

We were just about home free, the cop was walking back toward the fence, when a kid a few years younger than me came bursting through the house onto the back deck. He didn't glance up from the bags in his hand, just set them on the table and began to rummage through them. The cop stopped to take notice of the kid.

"Pops, they didn't have the kind you wanted. But they had this other brand with the state of Florida on it. It's slim pickings in the stores in this po-dunk town so you'll have to deal with the cigarettes I could find. Fred do you guys have any…" The kid stopped mid sentence when he realized that Fred and Meryl weren't alone. His eyes landed on Dre and then me as he stood frozen in shock.

"Hey kid," Beaman called out. The kids head snapped to the officer.

"Uh, yeah?" He asked, holding his hands in the air as if he were under arrest.

"Fuck," Fred muttered.

"You been here all day?"

"Yeah, sure have," the kid answered.

"Fuck," it was my turn to mutter.

"Those two been here all day?" He asked, looking downright triumphant as he pointed to me and Doc. She squeezed my arm.

"Uhhh, yeah, man. It's been a party up in here," the kid

responded without skipping a beat. He laughed like a stoner in a movie would and lit a cigarette. "I just made a smoke run."

"Tell me, if they've been here all day. What are their names?"

The kid smiled and tapped on his head with his open palm as if he were trying to will out a memory of an introduction that never took place. "Ah man. I didn't catch the girl's name. First time I met her was tonight and I've had a lot of beers." he turned to Dre. "Sorry, I'm not real good with names."

"Alright then. What's his name?" The officer asked, pointing to me. Fred sat up straight and Meryl was just about to interject as the kid scratched his head and yawned like he was questioned by police on a daily basis and the entire thing was boring him to death.

I think I almost drowned when he said. "Oh, him? That's Preppy, but don't fucking ask me what his real name is cause I don't fucking know. Everyone just calls him Preppy or Prep. Is this some sort of weird test?" He took a seat at the patio table. "Am I on a hidden camera show?" He ducked his head and inspected the inside of the open table umbrella.

By the time he'd pulled his head out the officer was gone.

"Holy fuck!" Fred exclaimed. "That was fucking great!"

"Why was he so scared of you?" Dre asked Meryl.

Meryl smiled and took a deep drag of his cigar blowing smoke rings into the air. "I'm the fucking state attorney!" he said and everyone broke out into a fit of laughter.

Everyone that is except me and the kid.

"Our newest accomplice here is Kevin," Fred introduced.

"How do you know my name?" I asked Kevin, holding off on joining Fred, Meryl and Dre in the toast they were sharing because of a nagging in the back of my brain that told me that there was something about this kid.

Something…familiar.

Kevin took a drag of his cigarette and shrugged nonchalantly. "I just know it," he said with a shrug of his shoulders. He ashed his cigarette directly into the center of the spa. All eyes turned to him and Dre gasped like she was realizing something I hadn't. "Maybe on the account of you being my brother and all."

Preppy went stiff beside me. "There's no fucking way you can be my brother. I don't even fucking know who my old man is."

"Neither the fuck do I. But you know that cunt of a mother you got?"

"Unfortunately,"

"Well, it's the same cunt of a mother I got."

CHAPTER TWENTY

DRE

"DO YOU THINK he's telling the truth?" I asked Preppy as I washed my hands in the kitchen sink.

"Probably. Don't see why anyone would lie about having her as their mother." He pressed his nose against the back of my neck and inhaled. I broke out in goose bumps. "I think it's cute that you put the cookies outside on the deck to cool," Preppy said, coming up behind me and pressing his body into mine.

"That's the way Mirna always did it and it's her recipe. Gotta do it right or it's not worth doing,"

"Another lesson learned in rehab?"

"No, I think that one was from American Ninja Warrior."

"Really?" Preppy asked excitedly pulling me tighter against him.

I laughed and shook my head. "Nooooo!" I exclaimed, swatting at him with the dishtowel in my hand then giving it one last rinse before laying it over the neck of the faucet.

"Look at you being all domestic. You're like the lady on that old show. What was it called? Leave it to my Beaver?"

"That would be Leave it to Beaver," I corrected.

"Shit, you're right, Leave it to my Beaver must have been

the porn parody." Preppy brushed the hair off my shoulder and pressed his lips against the curve where my neck and shoulder met, trailing them across my prickled skin to the special place behind my ear that caused me to press my ass back into him and the hardness prodding at my lower back. I tilted my head to give him more access.

Preppy's beard tickled my skin as he kissed and licked every spot he knew made me greedy for more. I was awash in tingles and flutters.

And HIM.

Always HIM.

My lips, my nipples, my pussy were all ready for their turn with his magical lips. But he was in no hurry. I tried to spin around but he held me in place by my waist. "Nuh-uh, Doc. I'm taking my time with you today." Preppy grabbed the hem of my pencil skirt, bunching it in his hands before slowly pulling the soft cotton up my legs. His fingers grazed the bare skin on the outside of my thighs, and I shivered.

I was wet, needy, and ready for him to just bend me over the sink and take what was his when I noticed something through the kitchen window.

Not something.

Someone.

Five fingers reached up onto the deck. "Shit! Look! There's someone out there!" I shouted, pointing to what I'd just seen. Preppy immediately stepped out from behind me and shifted our positions so he was standing protectively in front of me. The thought of an intruder had me at full panic mode until the curious look on Preppy's face had me thinking that my panic may have been a little premature. He turned me back to the window and pointed at the hand. He smiled. That's when I took a closer look and noticed that the fingers were tiny and attached to an equally tiny and chubby hand and arm. I couldn't see the top of our little guests head as they blindly patted down the deck, they must have been on their tip-toes as he or she continued to feel around the deck until their hand landed on top of the plate of Mirna's famous chocolate chip cookies. First one cookie disappeared and then another, the cookies almost bigger than the hand of the thief stealing them. Preppy walked over to the slider and quietly dragged it open. I followed him as he crouched down next to the plate, our guest not even realizing we were there until Preppy spoke.

"Hey little dude, you got good taste in cookies. Those are the best in the world."

The kid stepped back and it was then I could see what Preppy already had. A little boy. No older than five or six years old. Skinny little thing with a dirty face and even dirtier dark brown hair, matted to the side of his head. He was swimming in a torn dress shirt three sizes too large, his sleeves covered his hands and the cookies in them when he dropped his arms and looked to the ground in shame. His jeans stopped just below his calves. The big toe on his left foot stuck out of his sneaker, which by the looks of it, was three sizes too small to begin with.

"You can have as many as you'd like, in fact I put them there just for you," I said in an attempt to make him feel less guilty than he looked. He remained silent but looked up at me with confusion in his bright blue eyes. "You live around here, right?" I asked, taking a stab in the dark. He nodded.

"Well I've seen you around and I thought to myself. I think

he would appreciate world famous chocolate chip cookies. Didn't I say that?" I asked Preppy.

"Uh. Yeah. Of course. As a cookie connoisseur myself I can recognize a fellow man who appreciate amazing baked goods." Preppy smiled and took a seat on the deck, his legs dangling down over the side. "Go ahead, man. Have at it. They're all for you. Surprised it took you this long to get here." The boy reluctantly lifted his arm, his sleeve falling to the crook of his elbow as he lifted the cookie to his mouth and took a small bite. His eyes never left Preppy's, as if he were asking permission during the entire time he chewed and swallowed that first mouthful.

"See? What I tell ya. Pretty damn good, right?"

The boy nodded enthusiastically and took another bite, this time managing to shove almost the entire cookie in his mouth in one shot, and then another and another until he'd downed at least four more in quick succession.

Preppy picked up one of his own and mimicked the boy, his teeth coated in chocolate when he spoke. "I'm Samuel Clearwater," Preppy introduced, extending his hand and swallowing hard. "But my friends call me Preppy." The boy looked at Preppy's extended hand like he's just produced a rattlesnake from his pocket. His eyes went wide and he took a step back. Preppy withdrew his arm and casually scratched the back of his head before and folded his hands together on his lap. He swung his feet like he was running in place.

"You got a name or am I just supposed to call you the cookie kid?"

The boy shrugged and my heart broke right then and there. I felt gutted. Whoever was supposed to be caring for this child wasn't doing much caring if ANY and immediately I felt the rage burning in my lungs because when Preppy asked him his name he didn't shrug like he didn't know it.

He shrugged like his name didn't MATTER.

I felt my eyes start to water. "You know what? I forgot to bring out the milk. I'm so sorry. You two boys chat for a second and I'll be right back," I said, standing up and running back inside.

When I was back inside and out of view of the boy and Preppy I took a second to lean over the sink and collect myself. Then I made several sandwiches with whatever I could find in the fridge and stacked them on a tray with two large glasses of milk. When I went back outside I set the tray on top of the step and took a seat next to it. "You know, Preppy. It was pretty funny how we made way too many sandwiches for lunch today."

Preppy immediately caught on and shot me a grateful smile. "Yeah, it's too bad they have to go to waste. Or hey," he turned to the boy who'd just polished off the last cookie. "I mean, I don't know if you're a sandwich guy too but these are just gonna go to waste so if you want…" the boy was already nodding.

I could see him eying the tray and thought he was going to make a full body lunge for it when he stopped and pointed at himself. He looked around the yard and then pointed to the lawnmower we'd parked next to the hose beside the deck.

Then he did it again, slower this time.

"You're trying to tell us your name aren't you?" I asked. He nodded and added a crooked toothed grin.

He again pointed to the lawnmower.

"I mean lawnmower is a strange name, kid. I'm not gonna lie. But we're in the south and I hate to tell ya, but I've heard stranger." Preppy leaned in and whispered with his hand on the side of his lips. "My third grade class had three Bubba's and I was in gym class with a kid named I

White Zombie. We'll just call yo

The kid waved at us, jumping

"That's your name isn't it?" I aske

He shook his head and positioned h

stretched and the other was by his cheek li

shoot an arrow. "Nah, his name is Bo!" Prepp

he'd just won Jeopardy. The boy jumped into the a

held up his hand for a high five but the second he saw the hesitation in his eyes he lowered it but kept the smile on his face.

Bo looked at me and then the tray. "Go right on ahead, Bo. Have as much as you want."

While he tore up the sandwiches Preppy and I shot each other "What the fuck are we gonna do about this poor kid" looks. I thought maybe he could be lost and we could help him find his way home, or maybe his family was down on their luck and homeless, migrating to towns like Logan's Beach in order to avoid the harsh weather further north when escaping the elements wasn't an option. I had a hundred reasons in my head why a little boy who presumably couldn't speak and who cowered at human touch, wandered into Mirna's backyard, dirty, starving, and completely alone.

His too big shirt fell off to one side exposing his collarbone and every indentation of his rib cage. My breath caught in my throat. There was no mistaking the mean looking purple and yellow bruise in the shape of a closed fist on his chest.

Preppy's eyes met mine and his nostrils flared. I saw the anger burning inside him that steam might as well have been coming off the top of his head. "So, where do you live?" I asked and suddenly Bo looked from me to Preppy and something about the [illegible] face shifted. He grabbed the last sandwich and [illegible] the yard, scurrying through a hole in the fence like [illegible] bunny being chased by a dog.

[illegible]eppy stood up and ran back into the house.

“Where are you going? We should go after him!” I shouted.

Preppy emerged a few seconds later with a gun in hand. He loaded it from the bottom, smacking the cartridge in place with his palm before cocking it to set one in the chamber. “I am going after him,” he said, tucking the gun into the waistband of his pants. “And the cocksucker responsible for him.”

CHAPTER TWENTY-ONE

DRE

PREPPY CAME BACK looking defeated. He wasn't able to find Bo but he was able to find something else. Bitterness.

I thought he was in the backyard but when I peeked out the window and noticed he wasn't there I went looking for him. I found him all right.

Sitting on the train tracks.

"Don't worry. We'll find him," I said, coming up behind him and wrapping my arms around his waste.

"We? That's fucking funny," Preppy muttered.

I released him and stood in front of him with my hands on my hips. "What the fuck is your problem?"

"Me?" He shook is head. "I don't have a problem. Oh, unless you mean these." He flung a stack of papers at my feet. I didn't need to bend down to pick them up to see that they were divorce papers. The return address was from a law office in New York.

Dad.

"What do you want me to say, Preppy? I didn't send these but apparently you think I would. They're from my dad. I told him what was going on. He jumped the gun. He thought he was doing the right thing."

"Maybe he is," he spat.

"Why would you say that?"

"Because I can't save him!" he shouted, jumping to his feet. "I can't save Bo. He's out there somewhere cold and he's alone or taking a beating and I can't save him. I can't take care of him and I can't take care of you."

"That's bullshit."

"No, that's fucking life. And you should go home, Doc. Go back to your dad before you realize there's nothing for you here."

"You don't mean that."

"I don't give two fucks what happens to me. I don't even know who I am to care about so how the fuck am I supposed to take care of you?"

"Samuel Clearwater, I might have needed you to take care of me once and you did. You saved my life. But I'm not that girl anymore. I can take care of myself. I can save myself if I need saving and if you need me to then I can save you too."

"Oh yeah? Just like you saved our baby?" he asked bitterly just as the lights of the train lit up the tracks and the side of Preppy's face. He looked to the train then back to me. Shaking his head as if I disgusted him.

"Take that back," I shouted as the train approached and the ground beneath us vibrated. The light grew brighter.

Preppy stood up but didn't step off the tracks. The train was seconds away. "I can't save you unless you want to be saved," I said. "Get off the fucking tracks! I won't have you die again! I won't!"

"Go home, Doc," Preppy repeated. Instead of stepping forward off the tracks he stepped backward onto the other side, the train missing him by inches. By the time it rolled by and I could see to the other side of the tracks, Preppy was gone.

Days went by with no sign of him. I let King and Ray know what happened and that he was missing again. We searched for him everywhere with no luck. My only hope was that he wasn't hurting himself or playing dodge-a-train again. Little did I know the decision to stay or go was going to be made for me. My phone rang and Edna was on the other end, sounding panicked.

"Edna, what's wrong?" I asked.

"It's your father...he had a heart attack."

"Is he..." The possibility too painful to even speak the word.

"They took him back a while ago. I have no idea."

"I'm on my way," I said, ending the call and grabbing my suitcase. I scribbled a note and left it on the counter just in case Preppy came back to the house.

I came to Logan's Beach for closure. Instead, I was leaving the same way I left the first time.

With a broken heart.

CHAPTER TWENTY-TWO

PREPPY

"RAY SAID YOU were back," King said from the doorway of the garage apartment. "She also said you were shit faced."

"She's goooooone," I sang. "Dre left and she's not coming back."

"I figured as much."

"So lemme ask you an important question," I slurred. "How much wood would a woodchuck chuck if a woodchuck could... fuck chuck." I held up my index finger. "Wait, who is Chuck and why is the woodchuck fucking him?" I slurred, sloshing amber liquid around in the bottle, missing my mouth entirely as I attempted to raise it to my lips. It dripped down my chin into my already liquor soaked beard. "I mean I'm not hatin' cause Chuck should be free to fuck who he wants to fuck, and all that jazzzzzz."

King folded his arms over his chest, the buckles on the thick leather belts he wore around his forearms clanked together. "Prep, you're fucking drunk."

I clucked my tongue. "That 'tis not be true, boss-man." I squinted after another fuzzier version of King appeared beside him looking identically as irritated.

"Bullshit," he scoffed, raising a scarred eyebrow down at me. "Don't fucking lie to me. You're off your ass wasted. I can smell you from here."

"Nopers, you are wroooong, sirrrrrr." I giggled, sounding like fucking chick, spilling more whiskey down my throat. I pointed toward my best friend with the neck of the bottle, it slipped from my hand and fell to the floor. I made an O shape with my mouth and my childish giggling turned into a fit of laughter as I slid down from the recliner and fell ass first onto the carpet. Deciding that the carpet, although now wet, was the softest and plushest thing I'd ever felt, I continued to slide down until I was flat on my back. I don't know how much time had passed, but when I finally looked up I found myself staring into two very angry sets of green eyes spinning around above me, like in one of those old cartoons where Bugs Bunny gets hit on the head and is suddenly being circled by little spinning blue birds.

"Yeah, not fucking drunk at all," both King's said sarcastically, crossing his arms over his chest. The belts around his forearms clanked as the buckles connected.

"Listen you two motherfuckers," I pointed between solid King to fuzzy King. "You're both wrong. I'm not JUST drunk." I placed a finger over my lips and lowered my voice to a whisper. I looked around as if someone might overhear me. "I is also very VERY fucking high."

"Pull your shit together, Preppy. We got kids around here now. I can't have you high at eight in the morning or stumbling around while they're fucking playing in the backyard." King pointed to the blow on the table. "You can't leave that shit around either. There is a safe in my shop and another hidden in the back closet. You can keep your stash there."

I sat up, his mention of the kids finding it's way through the haze and waking up a small part of my brain. "I've missed so fucking much," I said, suddenly feeling a sadness wash over me. I wiped my runny nose with the back of my hand and realizing there was white powder residue on the back of it I licked it off. I shook my head. "I've missed everything."

"Not everything, Prep," King said crouching down next to me. "But you can fix that. Look out that window. Look at those kids. Go meet your nieces and nephew. Go talk to Bear's girl and get to know her. Go insult Bear for fuck sake. I thought he was all torn up when we thought you were dead but I think he's more torn up now that you're back because you ain't you."

"What the fuck does Bear know. I'm me. I'm fucking fine."

King ran his hand over his hair and squinted as if he were in pain. "You know I really told myself that you were okay. That everything was going to be fine. I think I told myself that because I wanted it to be. But shit's not fine, Prep. You need help or time or something. Whatever this shit is that you're doing isn't working. You need to be able to get through whatever it was you've been through. If you can't talk to us and tell us what happened, then you need to talk to someone to help you get through it."

"I don't want to talk about it. Not with you. Not with anyone. I don't even want to talk about it with myself. It never happened. It's over," I slurred, reaching for the bottle and sticking my tongue into the neck to reach the last speck of un-spilled liquor clinging to the top.

King grabbed the bottle from my hand and slid it across the room, out of my reach.

"Give that back, motherfucker," I demanded, reaching my hand out and wagging my fingers at my lost bottle of booze.

"You think you've been through some shit? Well, you're not the only one. Ray was raped by Isaac right before he, or one of his men, shot you. She was kidnapped by her ex who played a round of 'burn off this tattoo' on her with a motherfucking blow torch. I was shot four times trying to save her. You want to hear some more shit? Just ask Bear what the fuck's been going on since you've been gone. Ask him about what Eli and his men did to him. I realize that you're fucking hurting but get your head out of your own fucking ass long enough to understand that you have people around you. Family. And we're here to help so stop fucking pushing us away."

"What the fuck happened to Bear?" I asked, sitting upright.

"Ask him your fucking self," King snapped.

"I would but everyone's been tiptoeing around me and no one fucking tells me anything!"

"Then get your ass up and come outside. Breathe some fresh air and at least try!"

I shook my head. "I want to. I really do. But I can't, man. I just can't. Every time I try to leave the light outside is blinding as fuck. Every time I convince myself it's all okay my chest seizes up and I…I just can't. And you're right. They don't need to be seeing me like this, so I'll go."

"Prep, that's not what I'm fucking saying and it's not what I want. That's not what any of us want. You been through hell. We get that. Let us help you through it. Come outside. Breathe some fresh fucking air and do something other than work on your uni-nostril."

I chuckled. "Was that your attempt at a joke?" I asked, lighting a cigarette and leaning back against the recliner. My temples started to ache with the beginnings of a headache.

"I guess," King said, scratching the back of his neck.

"It was fucking awful."

"Fuck off." King smiled, grabbing my face in his hands. "At least try, Prep. Try for us."

"I don't know if I can," I said honestly.

King surprised me by stomping back across the room and pulling me up by my arm. "Come on," he said dragging me into his shop and pushing me down onto the couch. He walked over to a picture on the wall and shifted it aside to reveal a safe. He entered a few numbers on the keypad and when the door opened his arm disappeared into the wall and when he pulled it out he was holding a notebook in his black gloved hands.

A familiar notebook.

He tossed it to me and I caught it. I didn't need to open it to know what it was. I ran my hand over my eleven-year-old doodling on the cover. SAMUEL CLEARWATER written in graffiti style letters over the top. "I can't believe you still have this," I said.

King reached over and turned to a dog-eared page, revealing the stilt home drawing we drew that first day on the playground. The day we met. The marker ink had barely faded. The drops of red from my bloody nose from being beat up minutes before were still visible over stick a figure version of ourselves. "Of course I fucking kept it. I don't want to forget where I came from or where I'm going." He pointed to the page. "THIS might have been two fucking kids making a plan, but I still live by what we wrote that day and god willing, far in the fucking future, I'll fucking die by it someday too. I want to know if you're still fucking with me."

I looked from the notebook to him. "We were just kids, Boss-man. We were just fucking around," I said, closing the notebook and tossing it up onto the tray.

King blew out a frustrated breath. "Preppy, since we were kids we've always said we were gonna go out into the world and we weren't going to wait for anyone to give us anything. We were gonna do what we wanted and take what we wanted. Since day fucking one, man. Me and you on that playground with that fucking notebook. We mapped out our lives in those scribbles. Don't tell me you don't fucking remember that and what it meant because I sure as shit do."

"I remember," I muttered, wondering where King was going with all this.

"You know; I don't think you fucking do remember." King stomped his way over to me, stopping only when his knees were pressed against mine, towering above me, glaring down as if he were about to strangle me with his bare hands. His nostrils flared. "You claim to remember. So tell me, what do we do when we want something?"

"We...we take it," I said, rubbing my temples and recalling the words the naive kid versions of ourselves wrote down that day.

"Louder," King demanded roughly grabbing me by the shoulders and lifting me off my feet.

"We take it." I said a little bit louder, pushing his hands off of me only to have him grip me again, harder this time, and step even closer until he was right up in my face and our noses were almost touching.

"Louder, motherfucker," King demanded with a growl.

"We take it!" I yelled, pushing against him only to have him push back against me yet again. He grabbed me by the back of the head and pushed his forehead against mine so he was staring right into my eyes and I had no choice but to stare back.

"Again! Louder! What do we do when we want something?" King screamed, anger pulsed from the vein in his neck as he talked through his teeth. "Tell. Me. What. We. DO!!!!"

I hit my boiling point. His fingers dug into the back of my neck as we squared off. "We take it!" I yelled. "We motherfucking take it! 'Cause it's ours! It's all fucking ours to fucking take!"

"Scream it! Show me you still fucking believe in this! In us!" King said shaking me by the back of the neck and screaming in my face.

"We fucking take it!" I roared back with everything I had, my teeth clenching together as King held his forehead against mine. "We fucking take all of it!!!!!"

King clapped me on the back and released me, but he continued to crowd my space, his eyes never leaving mine. "Good. Now tell me what happens when someone stands in the way of us taking what's ours?" He grabbed the notebook and thrust it against my chest. I closed my hands around it and looked from it to my best friend with new found determination I felt building in my soul.

"We fucking kill 'em'," I huffed feeling more like myself in that moment than I had since before I went into the hole.

"Damn fucking right we do," he said with a satisfied smile and another slap to my back. He pulled me in for a one armed hug before pushing me back down into the chair and turning around to pick up his stool. He placed it upright and sat back down, rolling back over to me and again picking up the needle.

"Now what?" I asked, feeling like he had more to say and wanting to hear it.

"Now? I'm gonna work on some of those scars of yours and you're gonna spend some time working on getting you right again. Whatever it takes."

"And then?"

King lit a joint and passed it to me. "And then you tell me."

A wicked smile spread across my face. "And then I'm going to get my fucking girl."

Bear stormed in with his helmet in hisl hand looking like he'd just driven his bike at break neck speeds. "Sorry to interrupt your little pow-wow," he turned to me, "but that kid you've been looking for, Prep? My boys found him."

I was instantly sober. "And?"

Bear shook his head and blew out a long breath. "And…it's not good, man."

CHAPTER TWENTY THREE

PREPPY

BEAR TOLD ME that Bo was in the hospital and my fucking heart sank into my gut.

Twenty minutes later I was staring at the nurse at check-in looked like she'd been on the wrong end of a beating herself. She had purple bruises on her face. One on her chin and the other under her right eye. I could tell she'd tried to cover it up with makeup, but no amount of concealer could cover those angry fuckers, and they were fresh, it would only get worse. "Car accident," she said when she saw me staring.

"Didn't know cars had fists," I commented.

She pursed her lips and set down the chart she'd been holding, looking me in the eye for the first time since I'd arrived. She sighed and looked around to make sure no one was listening. She lowered her voice to a whisper. "The boy you're looking for was brought in a few days ago with a minor concussion and a sprained wrist. He'd been banged up pretty badly and from what I could tell, pretty often. It's not the first time he's been in here either. Between you and me I called child services, but when I brought the social worker to his room he was already gone."

"You let him go?" I asked through my teeth, stretching my fingers to ease the tension building in my hands.

"Let him go?" She looked stunned at my question, hugging her clipboard to her chest. "We didn't lose him, he escaped."

"Do you have a home address for him?" I asked leaning over to look at the chart in her hand. "Please, I have to find him."

"You know damn well I can't tell you that," she whispered.

I was about to ask her nicely, beg her until she gave in, but the fluorescent lights overhead caught the yellowing edges of her bruises I thought of something else. "The same thing is happening to him that's happening to you. I recognize a good ass kicking when I see one. Shit, I've started thousands in my life, but I've got this crazy idea that I only start fights with someone who deserves it, someone who can fight back."

"I can't..."

"No, just listen. You see, that little boy? That was me. Years ago in another life I was the one with the concussion and the broken wrist. The one who'd been beaten and starved regularly."

"We've...we've all had problems," she said, backing up when I stepped into her space. I put my hand beside her head onto the wall and leaned in close.

"Yes, we all do. And right now my first problem is finding Bo so I can keep him safe. Do you want to know what my second problem is?" I asked.

She nodded.

"My second problem is that I'm going to find the person responsible for hurting him."

"What are you going to do when you find them?" she asked, sounding both scared and intrigued.

"That leads me to my third problem. Body disposal."

She gasped but didn't move away.

"What if I could promise you the same thing?" I whispered.

"What?" she asked, her eyes going wide.

I grabbed a post-it tacked to the bulletin board above her head and grabbed her pen out of her hands. "Write down Bo's address. Underneath it, write the name and address of the cocksucker who did this to you." I shrugged. "And I'll dig an extra hole."

She grabbed the paper and pen from my hands. "I don't know what you're talking about. There is no one hurting me. I told you. I got in a car accident." She smiled at another nurse walking by and dropped it the second she was gone. "But I'll give you the address of the boy so you can get the fuck out of here and leave me alone." She scribbled on the paper and handed it to me. "It's not so much of an address as it is a location. We don't have any official address on file for him but one of the other nurse's said they see him around there from time to time."

"Thank you," I said, turning to leave.

"Go save that boy," she called out.

I waited until I got to the parking lot to check the post-it in my hand. She'd written Bo's location down all right.

And more.

Check the Rainbow Ends Trailer Park for your boy
Trip Reid
1720 Alabaster Road Apt 4
Black hair. Snake tattoo on his forearm.
Mean right hook..
He's always home...Thank you.

King, Bear and I scoured the trailer park for any sign of Bo, but he couldn't be found. Some of the neighbors pointed us in the direction of a mound of garbage. We wouldn't have even known a trailer was underneath if we hadn't been told. I pushed over a stack of empty cans with my foot and was about to kick in the door when a tall man with bloodshot eyes and a beer in his hand approached us.

"Word is you're looking for the kid?" he asked, adjusting the brim of his trucker hat depicting the silhouette of a stripper sliding down a pole.

"Yeah, we're looking for him. You Bo's dad?" King asked, stepping in front of me, and for good reason. I was wound so tight I would have fired first and asked questions later. The funny thing about dead men was that they didn't talk and we needed this shit bag to tell us where Bo was.

"Names Buck. I'm the boys step-dad," he corrected, crossing his arms over his bare chest that was covered in paper clip style prison tats.

"Fucking figures," I muttered.

"What the fuck do you want with him?" Buck asked. "He steal something from you?" He leaned to the side, spitting black tobacco onto the asphalt. He wiped the spittle off his chin with the back of his hand. "I told that boy to quit stealing shit. I guess that woopin' I gave him last time didn't teach him any kind of lesson. Looks like he's got another one comin'."

My rage had reached the point of no return and King felt it too because he stepped aside and let me come forward. "The only thing he stole was food. And while I'm sure your cigarette and beer money comes first you could have bothered to feed your fucking kid."

"Who the fuck are you to tell me how to discipline my kid? Withholding supper builds character. It's how my daddy and his daddy before him did it and it's how I do it."

"So the bruises and beatings are all part of it too?" I asked.

"If the boy won't answer my questions, he gets punished."

"Wait, he can't speak...so you gave him a concussion? Starved him?"

"What the fuck?" Bear asked.

"Can't speak or won't?" Buck asked, crushing the empty beer can in his hand and tossing it onto the pile beside the door. "Should have never bothered with the boy or his whore of a mama. Hope wherever he is he don't come the fuck back or he's gonna get the tail end of a switch and learn what real punishments all about." He shook his head. "If you want the little retard so much you can fucking have him."

"Where the fuck do you think you're going?" I asked, blocking his way back into the trailer.

Buck looked over my shoulder to the crowd of neighbors that had gathered around to watch the commotion. Buck sneered, tobacco covered his yellow teeth.

"What are you gonna do? Call the fucking pigs? IF they even bother to arrest me I'll do thirty days at most and be out fucking his mama again before football season starts." Buck laughed.

"He must be new in town," King said from somewhere behind me.

"'Real new. 'Cause we don't call cops," Bear added, pushing his gun into my hand. As soon as I touched the cold metal I knew it wasn't his gun after all. It was mine. "We didn't get rid of all of your shit," Bear said to me.

"What? You gonna shoot me in front of all these people? You

gonna kill me in the middle of the fucking day with a bunch of witnesses standing around who could send you to jail?" Buck rolled his eyes.

"He really must be new in town," Bear joked.

I raised the gun and aimed it at Buck's chest.

"Why do you keep saying that!" Buck screamed backing up and raising his hands in the air. He looked over my shoulder to the crowd where not one person was making a move to protect him.

"Because," I said, cocking the gun. "None of them are going to call the fucking cops."

"Oh yeah?" Buck challenged "And why the fuck is that?"

I pulled the trigger twice, sending Buck's bleeding body rolling into a heap of his own garbage.

"Because, unlike you, they know who we fucking are."

I may not have found Bo, but I did find someone else. An old friend of mine I didn't even know I missed.

And his name was Revenge.

"Reunited and it feels so goooooood," I sang out the open truck window as we flew over the causeway. I breathed in the salty air and it wasn't enough. I opened my mouth so I could taste it on my tongue. Bear pulled me inside by my shirt. "Fuck, that was better than any therapy," I said after planting my ass back on the seat. "What a fucking rush!"

"Yeah, Prep, if it put you in this good of a mood we should find someone else to kill," Bear said.

I pulled the note from my pocket and smiled. "Done."

"'Bout time you started feeling better," King said, turning onto the dirt road under the bridge.

"No!" I exclaimed, turning toward them and gesturing with my hands as I spoke, one of which was still holding the gun. MY gun. “I don’t just feel better; I feel…” I looked up at my two best friends who were eagerly awaiting for me to tell them something the shit eating grins on their faces told me they already knew.

“ALIVE. I feel fucking *ALIVE*.”

CHAPTER TWENTY-FOUR

DRE

FIVE MONTHS LATER

I PULLED THE COVERS up to my chin but was still unable to shake the chill that had seeped into my bones. Every single degree the temperature dropped made me miss Logan's Beach even more than I already did.

When I realized the chill was coming from my bedroom window that I didn't remember leaving open I wrapped my blanket around my shoulders and padded over to shut it, sleepily bumping into my desk in the process.

"You look like an adorable fucking eskimo," a deep voice said from out of nowhere. I turned around and jumped back, bracing my hands on the window sill as the door slowly creaked closed. A face I never thought I'd see again stepped out from the shadows. He smiled and his eyes gleamed.

"What?" I asked. "Why are you here?"

"Why wouldn't I be here?" he asked like it was an absurd question, and I wasn't sure if he was telling me that was the reason he was there or just stating a fact.

"Because it's been five months and I haven't heard a damn thing from you," I said, trying to catch my breath. Preppy walked around the room slowly picking up frames and trophies from my youth and running his hands over my ribbon for winning first place in the eighth grade science fair. "You scared the shit out of me you know."

"How's your dad?"

"He's fine now. It was minor heart attack. He just has to watch what he eats and his stress levels. He was lucky he noticed the signs as early as he did and Edna called for help," I said.

"That's good. What did you make to win this?" Preppy asked. He held up the ribbon.

I mashed my lips together. "A portable printing press."

"For books and shit?" He set the ribbon back down.

I shook my head and wrapped the blanket around me tighter. I shivered, but this time the cold had nothing to do with it. "A money press."

Preppy smiled and I saw pride gleam in his eyes. "You made a counterfeit money printing press in the eighth grade...and you won?"

I shrugged. "Wasn't that hard. Second place was one of those volcanoes that dripped tomato soup from the top." Preppy was quiet as he approached the bed where he stood on one side and I stood on the other.

"Why are you here?" I asked.

"The divorce papers," Preppy said.

My heart sank. "So you came here to deliver them in person?"

Preppy reached into his back pocket and pulled out a manilla envelope. "Something like that," he said, opening it and spilling paper confetti onto my bed between us. "More like bring them back."

Preppy was silent as he paced the room, tugging at his hair.

A vein pulsed in his neck. I couldn't help but notice that he'd gained a substantial amount of weight since I'd last seen him. Mostly muscle. His biceps flexed under the fabric of his white button down. This was no longer skinny-lean Preppy. He might have been lean but when his arms lifted over his head and he let out a deep sigh I couldn't help ogling his ab muscles outlined by his shirt.

That's also when I realized that for the exception of a missing bow-tie he was wearing typical Preppy attire. Suspenders, khakis, boots. His hair had grown into the style I remembered from years ago, long on the top, shaved on the sides.

My insides clenched but my mind raced along with my heart. I couldn't take it anymore.

"What do you want?" I screamed, literally pulling at the roots of my hair and charging him across the mattress until I was on my knees on the bed eye to eye with the man who'd broken my heart on more than one occasion. It was a good thing my dad was out. "You have to tell me what you want!"

He stood his ground and shouted back. "I want YOU!"

"Then let me the fuck in!" I yelled through gritted teeth, shoving against his chest. "Tell me what happened to you and let me the fuck in!"

Preppy growled. "He fucking tortured me!" he screamed, his face turning red with his anger, a vein pulsed in his throat. I gasped and sat back on my feet, watching as his walls finally crumbled. "Is that what you want to fucking hear? Do you want to know about all the times he beat me with a bat, waited for my injuries to start to heal, before doing it all over again on top of the bruises? Do you want to hear how sliced me with a sharp knife until my skin was shredded?" His voice grew lower, darker.

"Or maybe you want to hear about how he sent one of his biker bitches down to fuck me in the ass in an attempt to fucking break me? You want to know how he sounded when he laughed as he came on my back? Or how he kicked me in my spine when he was done and I blacked out when my head hit the fucking wall because I couldn't even hold myself up." Preppy looked to the sky and then back to me. "I couldn't hold myself up never mind fight him off even though I tried. I fucking tried!"

"Preppy…"

"No, I don't need or want your fucking pity." He quieted sinking to his knees on the carpet and I slid down from the bed onto mine, craning my neck so I could look into his eyes. "I have nightmares all the time. You know what's the only thing that makes them go away?" He placed his hand over mine. "You. You silence the world when it's too fucking loud. You make me feel less broken."

"You're not broken!" I said, grabbing his hands in mine and away from his face. He opened his eyes. "You're not broken."

"I'll always be a bit broken," he said, staring at me with glassy eyes.

"That's bullshit," I said. I released his hands and stood up abruptly. I pulled open my desk drawer and retrieved the proof I needed. I unfolded the wrinkled piece of paper and stalked back over to him shoving it into his hands. "A broken man didn't write these words."

"You got my letter," Preppy said, turning the page in his hands, the ink smudged with the millions of tears I'd cried reading his words a thousand times over and over again. A small smile appeared on his face. "You lied to me, Doc," he said, sounding both amused and pissed off.

"I did. I didn't tell you because I didn't know if you still felt the same and I didn't want to make assumptions when you were in a shitty place."

His voice softened to a whisper. "Do you want to hear about how the only fucking reason I survived that place was by thinking of you every single fucking day and night. I even meditated like Mirna showed me and tried to go somewhere in my mind, anywhere that wasn't there. I spent hours in my head having fake conversations with my friends. With you. I don't remember much, just wanting to get away. I'm alive because of you."

"No, you're alive because you're YOU. Because you battled with the reaper and you won. Because you're Samuel fucking Clearwater and you make your own rules." I laughed and choked on a sob. Preppy smiled. "That place you went to in your mind? It was home. It was to your family. To me. I heard you. We all did. Me. King. Bear. Ray. Even Thia."

"You really believe that?" Preppy asked, raising a brow and brushing a hair from my face.

"Yeah. As crazy as it sounds, yeah, I think I do."

Preppy leaned in close, pulling my lips within an inch of his. "You always were a little fucking crazy," he breathed. He leaned down to kiss me and I pulled away. I stood up and walked to the other side of the room.

"You made me think you were dead again. I can't live in a constant state of fear that you're going to be hurt or worse. I just can't. You broke me and I can't."

"You're the one who taught me that. If you're hurting, you don't have to stay hurting. I'll take your hurt for you. I'll take it all for you. I'd go back down in that fucking hole all over again if it meant getting to see you just one last fucking time. I'm a selfish fucking man and when it comes to you I'm the most selfish man of them all, because I want you regardless of the fact that I'm no good for you."

"I don't..." I started, but stopped when I realized I had no clue what I was going to say.

His eyes spoke volumes of how he was feeling. Sad, but determined, rimmed in red, but wide open and clear. "And if this is all coming to an end before it even has a chance of beginning again then there's no fucking risk in telling you what I have to tell you now. What I have to say to you before it swallows me fucking whole."

I shook my head, both fearing and anticipating what was coming next. But nothing could've prepared me for those three little words that trampled over me like a herd of fucking cattle.

"I love you."

I shook my head again, not to disagree, but to shake the words from my brain. Words he couldn't have really said. It was either my imagination or lies. They had to be. Either way, my heart couldn't take much more. The barely held together seams of the last mending had started unraveling the second I saw him in that bed. ALIVE. And with those three little words that held so much power I felt them reach down my throat into my chest and start snipping away at the fraying threads stitch by stitch. "No. No, you can't just love me." I heard myself choke out. "You just think you do because now I belong to someone else," I rationalized. "And you want what you can't have."

"Fuck that," he said, anger lacing his words. His eyebrows pointed inward causing lines on his forehead to appear. "You think I just decided NOW that I loved you?"

"Well, maybe I don't love you."

"Doc, this wasn't a revelation 'cause you showed up with Justin Bieber's stunt double and I thought you were engaged. I love you because I fucking love you. I've loved you since way back before I fucked it all up, you know, the first time. I thought if I pretended to be happy that I'd be happy but it took months of sitting in the dirt being tortured every single fucking day to realize that the real torture was not telling you how I fucking felt from that very first day."

"You..."

"I loved you when I carried your broken body to Mirna's that first time. I think I even loved you from the second I saw you up on that water tower. You were so broken...and so fucking beautiful."

"When you saved me," I said, unable to yet find my voice it came out as a whisper.

Preppy shook his head. "No, when you saved ME." I gasped and placed my hand over my chest where I was sure I was about to pass out from the pain. Tears welled up in my eyes and rolled in warm drips down my cheeks to my chin. Preppy reached out and wiped the tear from my chin with his thumb. He then placed his own hand over his chest like he was feeling the same kind of unraveling I was. "And before you say anything else. Before you tell me that I can't really love you, or to fuck off, or that you don't feel the same way, I have to tell you first, that I don't like being lied to."

"Who lied to you?" I asked, trying to look anywhere but into his eyes, but it was impossible. I was locked into his determined gaze.

"You did, Doc. You fucking lied to me," he growled.

"When?"

"Twice actually. First, when you told me you didn't love me." Preppy took a step forward, and I instinctively took a step back. He chuckled low and deep. "Because you and I both know it's bullshit."

"And the second time?" I tried to swallow down the lump forming in my throat that was threatening my airway, causing me to breathe erratically. My chest heaved up and and down with the need to catch my breath.

He smiled wickedly. "Then when you said I couldn't have you."

"Why…why all this? Why now?" I asked.

"Because, Doc. When I was still in that fucking hole I made a promise to myself that I was going to find you. Find us again. What I didn't realize was that before I could do that, I had to find me first and there wasn't anything you or anyone else could do to push that along."

"Did you find you?"

"Fuck yeah, I did."

"Therapy?"

"Something like that."

"Now come home. We've got something else we got to take care of. Together."

"What's that?" I asked, my heart still fluttering like a schoolgirl.

He reached in his back pocket and handed me a stack of papers. "We found him. We found Bo. He's been living with me at the house for a while. Doc, I don't want him to have the same life as me. I see me in him and I think we can still save him. Just got to get his useless mama to sign these."

Application for Adoption of Minor Child was the heading.

I leapt into his arms and nodded. Tears spilled down my face. "So what do you say, Doc?" He asked. "You wanna be my baby mama?"

I scrunched up my face like I had to think about it. "Are you going to keep me this time?"

Preppy smiled from ear to ear. "Yeah, Doc. And I'm never fucking letting you go," Preppy said. He reached behind him and took off his shirt in that way that only men can do. I gasped when he leaned over to the nightstand and flicked on the lamp.

"Wow," I said. When I noticed Preppy's muscles under his shirt it was nothing compared to seeing them tight and perfect without his shirt. And although his ridiculous body had me foaming at the mouth that wasn't what I was staring at. The wound on his side. The one from the gunshot. The one that healed wonky and left a criss crossing of scars across his torso had been tattooed over by a large intricate colorful piece that had me in tears all over again. Red lips. Glasses. Pencil skirt. Even the bow tie heels Mirna had given me. "It's me," I gasped.

"So you gonna answer me or just lay there drooling?" he asked with a wink. "You coming home?"

"Yes. I'm coming home," I said and the warmth on Preppy's face was enough to melt away and fears or doubts I might have had.

"Good, now we can get to the part where we fuck," he said, and his mouth came down over mine.

"Wait, where are we going to live? Mirna's house already sold. I sent the keys down months ago," I said.

"More fucking, less talking," Preppy said, tossing me onto the bed.

Who was I to argue?

He didn't waste any time, hooking my booty shorts and panties and dragging them off my legs, tossing them to the side. Without hesitation he pushed my thighs apart and dove in. The second his tongue made contact with my clit I moaned long low and LOUD.

"I missed this beautiful pussy," he said against me, the vibrations of his words mixed with the circular tongue motion was bringing me closer and closer to the edge.

I was about to come, I could feel it right there, just a few more long strokes of Preppy's talented tongue and I… heard my dad come in from his bowling league game. "Andrea?" He called out, but Preppy didn't stop. Not only did he not stop he pushed a long thick finger into my ass and I squealed. He reached up and covered my breast with his hand, pinching hard on my nipple. "Are you home? Bowling sucked. We lost to that group of women in their eighties again. I'm pretty sure we're going to be last again this year."

"Answer the man," Preppy said against my folds. He pulled out his finger only to push it back in.

"I'm here dad. I'm just…really tired so I'm just going to go to bed early," I shouted back. Preppy thrust his tongue inside me and I arched my back.

"Yeah, I'm beat too, see you in the morning," he said, I heard his door close and the second it clicked Preppy increased his efforts, relentlessly fucking my pussy with his tongue and my ass with his finger until I grabbed a pillow, smashed it over my own face, and screamed out my orgasm into goose down.

It was Preppy who eventually took the pillow off my face. "Thought you were suffocating under there," he laughed.

"You're such a shit," I said.

He settled between my legs and pushed his entire massive length inside of me in one quick thrust. I was about to scream out again but he put two fingers in my mouth. "Bite down on me if you need to, but don't make a sound, Doc," Preppy said wickedly.

At first he built a slow rhythm again reaching behind me and pushing a finger into my ass which heightened everything his cock was doing in my pussy. He was making it impossible not to scream so I did what he said and I bit down on his hand. "That's it, bite me. Show me how much you want to scream."

I bit down harder and he responded by thrusting even harder. I was so wound up that when he bent down and bit my nipple I was already coming, the pleasure so great I was lost to anything but me and Preppy and the greatest fucking orgasm.

Preppy pulled out, coming in long hot streams of white over my neck and tits, claiming me, marking me, making me his.

Keeping me.

CHAPTER TWENTY-FIVE

DRE

It was a good thing I was wearing a seatbelt because if I hadn't been strapped down in the back seat I would've hit my head on the exposed metal roof of Billy's van at least a dozen times as we navigated down the pothole infested street.

I put my arm across Bo's shoulders and held him tighter to me. His own seatbelt might have been buckled but they were made for people of a certain size, not age. Bo might have been six years old but his belt was doing jack to actually keep him safe.

"He needs a booster seat," I pointed out, trying to distract myself from anything other than where we were headed or the task at hand. For that moment it was transportation safety.

Preppy was in the passenger seat. He turned around and eyed the loose belt around Bo's waist. "On it," he said, pulling out his phone and quickly tapping on the keys. "Ray says she has an extra."

Bo took that moment to smile up at me. I could feel his nervousness radiating off of him almost as much as I could feel my own. I saw it in the way his eyes shifted from object to object in the van like he was trying to find something to focus on yet when he smiled up at me it was if he were trying to comfort me, instead of the other way around.

Which was good, because I needed it.

My guts were twisting over and over again. I swallowed the bile rising in my throat as I wrung out my sweaty hands on my lap. The uneasy feeling only getting worse as we turned from the bumpy road into an even bumpier one past the rusted sign falling from the post that told us we were entering the trailer park.

From the back seat I could see Preppy's entire body go completely stiff as we rolled past one dilapidated trailer after another.

Junk was piled high in front of almost every site. A middle aged couple stood in the middle of the road between a section of four trailers parked at angled facing one another. They didn't budge when they saw us coming so Billy turned the wheel and maneuvered around them. The man was shirtless, wearing nothing but light colored jeans that were folded open at the fly as he chugged from a bottle wrapped in a brown paper bag. He flicked us off as we passed. The woman, who was wearing a stained lavender tank top and a pair of cotton underwear, scowled although I wasn't sure if it was meant for us or the man she was arguing with. When we'd passed them by I continued to watch out the back window. The man had turned his back on the woman and that's when she leapt onto him, wrapping her arms and legs around him tightly and screaming in a high pitch tone that made me grateful the windows were rolled up. The bottle fell from the man's hand and rolled across the street as he stumbled for balance, it was the last I saw of them before we rounded the corner and they disappeared from view.

Bo was looking out the window as well although he seemed unfazed by the couple. It was when we turned that he reached for my hand and squeezed tightly, his little fingernails pressing down hard into the skin of my palm. He leaned against me and snuggled his face into my arm as he weren't cutting off my circulation where our hands were joined.

He could squeeze as hard as he wanted. I took a deep breath. I wasn't going to pull away.

Not then.

Not ever.

I had silently questioned why Billy was tagging along with us until we pulled up to our destination, a dimly lit trailer in the back of the park, and it dawned on me that Billy must have been there to keep an eye on Bo because there was no fucking way he was going to come inside with us. I wasn't going to ever let him back inside that thing.

Ever.

Preppy hopped out of the van and I gave Bo's hand a squeeze when the door was rolled open. "We'll be right back. Stay with Billy, okay?" Preppy asked, holding out his fist for Bo to bump, which he did.

I got out and we rolled the door closed. Billy saluted Preppy as we turned toward the crumbling pile of aluminum in front of us. It looked like a junkyard and smelled like an open sewer. Pizza boxes, eggshells, fast food wrappers with flies buzzing over it littered the small sidewalk to the front steps. The smell of urine burned my nostrils as we approached the door.

"Are you ready for this?" I asked Preppy as he took my hand and raised it to his lips to give it a quick kiss.

"Fuck no." He opened the door without knocking and stepped inside.

Bo's MOTHER, FOR lack of a better term, was named Trish. She didn't stand up when we'd entered and I wasn't sure if it was because she couldn't or just didn't want to. She was tiny and frail, perched on a tattered recliner with a knitted blanket with so many holes in it there was no way it served any kind of purpose. "Hope you two know that you'd be the ones getting a bum deal. Kid don't even talk. Might even be a retard," she said, looking from me to Preppy like we were the crazy ones.

I was FUMING in a way I'd never felt before. Preppy must have sensed my anger because he reached out and grabbed my arm like I was going to lunge at her and I can honestly say that I was definitely thinking about it. I answered her through my teeth, "Have you ever thought that unlike some people who just run their fucking mouths without a single thought behind their words, that maybe Bo's just waiting for something important to say?"

"Whatever, as long as you know what you're getting into," she said, scratching at the scabs on her arm, a drop of blood bubbled to the surface and trickled down to her wrist and then into the lines of her palm but she didn't seem to notice. "So how much?"

"You want us to BUY him from you?" Preppy asked in complete disbelief, although something told me that he wasn't as surprised as his voice led on. "You've got to be fucking kidding me?" It was his turn to be angry. The chords in his neck tightened. He reached into the waistband of his pants and pulled his gun, holding it with two shaky hands as if it were physically hurting him not to pull the trigger.

Trish barely flinched when she looked up and saw the silver barrel pointed down at the top of her greasy grey head. He cocked the gun, the click echoed throughout the small room. He stepped forward, glaring hatred down at the ghost of a woman as he pressed the gun to her forehead. "You give him a shitty fucking life in this open sewer of a home. You starve him. Neglect him. And do God-knows fucking WHAT to him and now you want to SELL him?" An evil sounding laugh escaped him. "Fuck, I've seen some evil shit in my life but right up there with the likes of my own fucking mother."

"And why shouldn't I get paid?" Trish asked, ignoring everything Preppy said that wasn't in line with what she wanted to hear. "You want something that's mine. In my world you gotta pay for what you want, supply and demand." She lit a cigarette butt with shaky hands and inhaled once before the cherry fell off into her lap, she brushed it off her blanket and it fell to the floor where she stubbed it out with her dirty bare foot.

"You treat him like a fucking nuisance dog and when we tell you that we're gonna take him off your hands for you all you can respond with is how much?" Preppy licked his lips like he could taste the kill in front of him. "I tell you what you stupid cunt, how about you sign those papers and I pay you by not blowing your motherfucking head off right now," he seethed.

"Prep," I said, using the calmest tone of voice I could muster. I knew that Preppy identified with Bo and the way he was raised and neglected, but looking down at this frail woman in the throes of heavy addiction I couldn't help but think that if things hadn't happened exactly the way they had I could so easily have ended up just like her. "Let me talk to her."

"Doc," Preppy started to argue, but he must have seen the determination written all over my face. "Three minutes, I'll be right outside," he said, with a look that said he didn't like the idea at all. With one last glare down at Bo's mother he lowered his gun to his side but didn't put it away before leaving, slamming the trailer door shut behind him.

"Trish, right?" I asked, taking a step into the living room over a pile of rags. I side stepped the couch and tried not to let the disgust show on my face as I saw thousands fleas jumping up from the rug as I maneuvered around the garbage, my ankles under instant attack as they landed bite after bite. I pushed on.

"That's right. It's Tricia but everyone calls me Trish."

"Heroin?" I asked, pointing to the needle on the side table.

Trish looked up at me for the first time as if she were just noticing I was there. "None of your fucking business. You think just because you're a stiff that you came come into my fucking home and take my kid for nothing? That you're some how better than me 'cause you're not depending on a fucking needle to get you through the day?" Trish shook her head from and lit the butt of another cigarette from the overflowing ashtray on the side table to next to her chair.

I stepped closer and knelt down next to her. I pulled up my sleeves and set my forearms across her bony knees. My touch startled her and she sat up as if I'd stabbed her. "I haven't always been a stiff," I said, using my eyes to point to the scars on the inside of my arms. "I know a lot more about how you're feeling then you think I do." Trish's gaze roamed my scars. Her eyes met mine. "I've been where you are. I know what it's like to have something so small take all the control when it comes to your life."

Trish looked like she was contemplating something. She sat back in her chair and I stood back up, pulling my sleeves back down my arms. She looked at her own arms then back up at me.

"So you think because you used to be a junkie that you can bully me into giving you my kid? Is that it?"

I shook my head. "No, I think that because you're a junkie you understand why he'd be better off living somewhere where your addiction isn't what he sees every morning and every night. Where heroin use won't be his normal. Where the fridge will be full and so will his belly. Where his clothes will be clean and he'll go to school every day. But most importantly, where he'll be loved and that love will be more important than anything. It will come first…" I glanced down to the needle and spoon on the table. "Before any needle."

Trish scoffed. "My love for him comes before…"

"Don't bullshit me," I interrupted. "That comes first, second, third…and only."

Trish's shoulders hunched over even more. With a growl she grabbed a pen off the side of the table and was about to sign her name to the page when Preppy opened the front door and said. "Wait," he said, throwing me off. I was about to ask him why when he turned and called for Billy who came in a second later carrying something in his hand. He walked over to Trish without looking around, without saying a word. I think it was the only time I'd ever seen him not smiling. He nodded for Trish to sign and when she was done he grabbed the pen from her hand. That's when I realized what he was holding was a stamp which he pressed down on bottom of each page. He initialed a few lines under her signature, and with a nod to Preppy on his way out he left without saying a single word.

I gathered the papers and handed them to Preppy who was still standing by the door.

"You're alright, kid. You know that?" Trish called out just as we were about to leave. "I knew you weren't going to let that one over there kill me." She flashed me a rotten toothed smile.

"You're right," I turned back around and glared daggers at the reason behind poor Bo's pain. I stared at her with all the hatred I could muster. "Because if you didn't sign the papers and do the right thing by Bo, then I would have killed you myself."

Trish had the audacity to laugh. "So much for understanding a fellow addict," she grumbled. "For a minute I thought you were like me. But you lied. You're just another stiff making threats to get what you want."

I grabbed Preppy's hand and turned back to Trish. "You're confusing understanding for sympathy. I understand what you're going through, but I hated myself when I was going through it and because of what you've put Bo through…I hate you even more."

Preppy helped me down the crumbling steps where Billy was waiting for us, leaning against the van.

"Hang on a sec," Preppy said, heading back up to the door, he opened it and disappeared inside, re-emerging just a few seconds later?

"What did you do?" I asked, although I was pretty sure he didn't kill her considering I hadn't heard any gunfire.

"She wanted payment for Bo," Preppy said, with a shrug. He opened the van door and I slid inside next to a sleeping Bo who was sprawled out across the bench seat. His chest rising and falling in slow rhythm. "So I gave it to her."

"You gave her money?" I mouthed, not wanting to wake up Bo.

Preppy smiled wickedly and with his hands on the roof he leaned into the van and whispered in my ear. "Nope. I gave her something she wanted more, and enough of it to almost guarantee she won't ever be a problem for us." Preppy kissed me on the cheek and slid the door shut, rounding the van.

Heroin. He'd given her heroin.

Preppy was right. As far gone as Trish was she wouldn't be able to resist. The chances of her surviving until the morning were slim to…she'd be dead by morning.

I waited for the familiar guilt that used to come all the time, even when it had no reason to. At any second I expected that inner voice of mine to tell me I shouldn't allow Trish to die.

Nothing.

By the time Preppy popped into the passenger seat and Billy started the van I couldn't stop the smile from creeping onto my face.

As we pulled out of the trailer park Bo stirred so I pulled him onto my lap and softly stroked his newly cut hair. I took one last look at the dilapidated trailer as we pulled out onto the road, grateful that Bo would never have to spend another second there, never mind another night. The thing wasn't fit for human habitation. Not for Bo. Not even for Trish.

Bo snored lightly. Preppy leaned back and brushed Bo's hair out of his eyes and with a loving look in his eyes he gazed down at his son.

Our son.

"I could've easily ended up just like her," I whispered, feeling the tears prickling behind my eyes. Relief and happiness filled me with each rotation of the tires that brought us further and further away from that trailer park.

"No, you could never have ended up like her," Preppy argued.

"You can't say that; you don't know that."

"You would never have ended up like her," he said again. "Not fucking EVER."

"How can you be so sure?" I flattened my hand over Bo's little cheek feeling the warmth of his skin against my palm. Preppy covered my hand with his much larger one, intertwining our fingers. I looked up to find his eyes glistening as they stared directly into mine. I felt his determination when he said, "Because I wouldn't have let you."

CHAPTER TWENTY-SIX

PREPPY

"I'M SORRY IT took me so long to visit," I said as I stood above Grace's grave, feeling my heart smack against my rib cage like it was angry with me for taking it along for the ride it never asked to go on, pounding against my insides to let him the fuck out.

Too fucking late, motherfucker.

"I didn't know if I'd ever see you again, but this isn't the way it ever went down in my mind," I stuttered a sigh, my throat tightened painfully— I was barely able to swallow. I shoved my hands into my pockets and pulled them right back out. I kicked at the neatly trimmed grass with my boot then dropped down to my knees. I leaned forward, resting my hands against the low tombstone that was more like a plaque than an actual stone. I needed to be close to her, or what was left of her. I cringed, willing away the image of Grace as a decaying corpse that kept flashing through my mind.

The sun began to set, casting a shadow over the small cemetery. A grounds keeper in coveralls rolled over a small green shade tent. He stopped a few plots down at a spot with no marking and tossed a shovel into the grass. With the toe of his heavy yellow work boot he clicked a latch at the bottom of each of the four metal posts, locking the wheels in place. When he paused to wipe his sweaty forehead with a rag hanging from his back pocket, he looked over and his eyes met mine.

"How you doing today, son?" he asked with a heavy Spanish accent. He shoved the rag back into his pocket and picked up the shovel, stabbing it into the ground. He started scraping off the top layer of grass, dumping it into an awaiting bucket.

I glanced down to Grace's plaque back then back up to the grounds keeper. "Not gonna lie, man. I could totally be a whole lot fucking better," I said, my voice shaking with my grief.

"Was that your mama?" he asked, gesturing with his chin to the plaque as he turned over another shovel full of grass into the bucket.

I nodded. "As close to one as I ever had."

He nodded and continued working. "Sorry for your loss. I know it may not help, but death is just a part of life. We all die. Some before others. After working here for thirty some odd years I can tell you that death is not something to be sad about. It is something to be celebrated." He put a hand to his chest. "In my culture, when a loved one passes, we throw a huge fiesta and we drink until we can't feel our faces and then we dance and we make love under the stars and then we drink some more until we can't feel the rest of our bodies. It's about joy. It's about celebrating life, not cursing death."

I leaned back and sat on my ass, not caring about grass stains for once. I picked at a few weeds, tearing them apart in my hands—tossing them back onto the ground. "For the first time in my life I can truly say that I'm not exactly up for a fiesta right now."

He paused his shovel and turned to face me, resting his chin on the wide handle. 'Diego' embroidered on the right breast of his faded coveralls. "Grief is normal, but you can't let it consume you." Diego pointed off into the distance, where just over the cracked sidewalk that ran through the middle of the cemetery a middle aged woman with short blonde hair wearing a short white dress crouched down over a grave and set down a bundle of blue carnations. "You see her?" he asked. The woman began to openly weep, her shoulders jostling, her eyes shut tightly, her mouth contorting and twisting as she laid down over the grave. The sounds of her sobs were picked up by the wind, spreading her sadness over the already depressing graveyard. "She's here every day at the same time— lays on her husbands grave and cries for hours and hours before she leaves, only to come back and do it all over again the next day. Always wears white like it's her wedding day."

"So?" I asked. "I mean it would be odd as fuck if she were doing it in the middle of the truck-pulls or at the bingo hall, but isn't crying kind of an expected thing at this place?" I shielded my eyes from the sudden presence of the sun peaking out from behind the slow passing clouds as it began to make it's final descent for the day.

"Her husband died seventeen years ago."

"Oh," I said.

"Yeah, exactly," He resumed his shoveling. "Once you let yourself get lost in it there ain't no returning from grief like that." He looked back over to the woman and shook his head. "That's why you need to celebrate and remember that you're still alive." He laid his shovel down and reached into a small red cooler, ice spilled over the sides as he pulled out a six pack of beer. "So what'll it be, son? We celebrating?" He jerked his head toward the woman in white. "Or are you gonna let someone else's death swallow up what little life you've been given on this earth?"

"Who the fuck are you?" I asked, feeling a smile tugging at the corners of my mouth. "You're like the fucking graveyard Tony Robbins or something."

He shrugged. "Or something." Diego raised the six pack in the air. "Choice is all yours man."

I glanced down at Grace's grave, to my MOTHER'S grave, and thought about what she would want for me and instantly I knew it wouldn't be sadness or tears. She always said she wanted me to be happy and in that moment I wanted to do anything and everything that she'd always wanted for me.

I jerked my chin up to Diego and held out my hands. "What the fuck are you waiting for?" His face lit up, a single gold tooth glinted as he underhanded the beer my way. I caught it, but just barely, fumbling with the cold wet cans as they almost slipped free from my grip. "Diego Martinez," the groundskeeper said, formally introducing himself as he sat down next to me and held out his hand.

"Samuel Clearwater," I offered, removing my hand from the beer and wiping it on my already grass stained pants before shaking the hand of my new alcohol providing grave digging life coach.

Diego and I celebrated that night. And by celebrated I mean that we got shit faced right there on Grace's grave. Not only did he have beer in that cooler but he also had a sizable bottle of unmarked tequila that I'm pretty sure he'd made at home in his bathtub because it tasted like pure gasoline. We were halfway through the bottle when the world faded away and I slipped into unconsciousness.

The warm rays of the sun woke me the next day and then proceeded to blind me as I opened my eyes just a sliver, letting in only a small amount of the already much to bright light. "Buh," I groaned. My own tongue tasted rancid, my mouth so dry it was as if I gargled with sand throughout the night.

I sat up slowly and blinked a few times to better adjust to the assault on my senses. When I was finally able to open my eyes I discovered that was still in the cemetery, still sitting over Grace's grave, but I was alone. There were no signs of Diego or his evil bottle of moonshine tequila, shovel, cooler, even the canopy he'd wheeled out the day before. The only sign he'd ever been there at all was the lingering hangover and the agony in my brain that felt as if an angry cat was using it as a scratching post.

"See you later, Grace." I whispered, resting my hand for a beat on her plaque and giving it a few taps before pushing to my feet. I took a few steps but then my head spun, the graveyard swirling around me. I paused and leaned on a nearby headstone to calm the spinning. After a few seconds I felt good enough to continue but when I straightened it was the name on the headstone I'd leaned on for support that caught my eye. "No fucking way," I said out loud as I ran my hand over the name engraved in the stone.

DIEGO MARTINEZ.

I rolled my eyes at myself. "It's a common fucking name," I explained to myself, which was totally true. In Southern Florida I couldn't swing my cock without hitting at least three Diego Martinez's. Then I read what was written below his name and I jumped back from it like it had shocked me. Maybe I'd suffered a lot more mental trauma by the hands of Chop then I'd realized because I was a few 'the sixth sense' moments away from printing out my own one-way ticket to one of those nice and cozy padded rooms with no windows.

Diego Martinez
Loving father, husband, grandfather.
Laid to rest in the grounds he cared for
lovingly for over thirty years.
Now watching over his hard work
from his place in heaven.
We celebrate his life.
May 5th 1944 - June 17th 2016

Delayed long term brain damage.

It was the only explanation for both the hallucinations and the pounding headache.

"Preppy…?" I loved hearing her say my name. I spun around to find the other person in the world who at times had me thinking I was going crazy. Because there, standing less than ten feet from me, wearing a strapless yellow sundress that flowed around her knees, was none other than the Doc herself, staring at me with a concern etched into her forehead.

"You by chance didn't see a grounds keeper around here did you? Grey coveralls? Looks like the guy from the Machete movies?"

She looked around the empty cemetery. "No…should I have seen him?" she asked slowly. Her focus dropped from my face to the grass stains on my jeans. "Are you okay?"

I held out my hand with my palm facing her. "Hang on. Gimme a sec, Doc." With my head still thundering I shut my eyes tightly and then open them again, sure enough Dre was still there, but since I was going crazy and all I didn't trust my own vision and needed more evidence. "I'm going to ask you a question and I just need you to answer it for me okay?" I took a step forward and Doc flashed me a small white toothed smile, doing a shit job of hiding the concern etched into her black corneas.

"Okay…" she said hesitantly.

"Just tell me the truth, Doc…are you really here right now?" I asked still not believing that my girl was finally home with me.

Dre looked down to her feet as if she were checking out to see where 'here' was. "Yeah, I mean. I think so."

"Just stay right there," I ordered, not wanting to get my hopes up before I had solid evidence. I held out my arms straight, locking my elbows in a very frankenstein-esque stance. I moved forward slowly and didn't stop until I smelled the lavender of her shampoo and my hands were resting on her shoulders. I squeezed my fingers, her soft skin was warm and very much alive beneath my touch.

"You really are here," I whispered, tipping up her chin so I could get a better look at the freckles on her nose.

"I'm really here," she said as if she really couldn't believe it herself.

"You're really here," I said again, interrupting her and giving her shoulders another squeeze.

"Satisfied?" she asked, her eyes locking onto mine. The air around us grew thick and charged. Suddenly, touching her shoulders wasn't enough.

When it came to Dre it would NEVER be enough.

"Fuck no. Not even close," I admitted, resting my forehead against hers. "What time is it?" I asked.

"It's time. Everyone's starting to show up at the house, even Kevin's coming," she said, pulling me by the hand. I still wasn't sure if the kid was my brother but he was enough of a delinquent to definitely give me reason to believe it was a possibility. "I have to go pick up my dad from the airport, but I'll be back. You sure you want to do this? Meeting the parents is kind of a big deal you know," she said, biting on her bright red lip.

"It is. And I'm totally sorry I can't introduce you to my parents but I don't know who my real dad is, King killed my stepdad, and my mother is a super cunt."

"Duly noted."

I nodded and she smiled brightly. I held onto her hand and let her lead me through the same cemetery I'd chased her through years ago. I didn't know where we were going, just that she had something to show me, but I decided that Dre could be dragging me through the gates back to hell and I wouldn't of cared.

I'd follow my wife anywhere.

"Oh, I almost forgot, you'll need this,: she said tossing me something soft. I knew what it was before I opened my hand. "I think it's time," Dre said.

I unfolded my palm and ran my thumb over the pink and yellow plaid of the bow tie in my hand. I smiled.

It was definitely fucking time.

CHAPTER TWENTY-SEVEN

DRE

MY FATHER TWISTED around in the passenger seat and with his mouth slightly agape he ran a palm over the the supple black leather in one slow appreciative motion of admiration like he was inspecting a stud horse. "You sure I can't keep it? I mean, it's not like he'd ever let you drive it. You're a terrible driver. Remember when you ran over Mrs. Stephens cat?" My dad teased with a wink.

"Excuse me?" I asked, raising my voice several octaves in mock offense. "If you remember I'd JUST gotten my driver's license that week! And not for nothing but I'll have you know that cat was suicidal."

"A suicidal cat?" my father asked, cocking an eyebrow.

"What else would you call it?" I lightly smacked the wheel. "That cat was mean as hell. And not to mention a hundred years old. And what black cat darts out across an unlit road in the middle of the night?"

"A suicidal one," my father deadpanned, but his straight face only lasted for a beat before his smile reappeared and he began to laugh, low and loud. It was a sound I hadn't realized how much I'd missed until right then.

It had been way too long.

"So OLD MAN, unless you want me to drive your side of the car into the causeway rails I suggest you be nice to your daughter about her driving skills," I teased back. "And NO you can't keep it," I said, patting the dashboard. "You did a great job on her, Dad. He'll love it and I promise that she'll be in good hands."

My father's laughter finally subsided. "I sure hope so, darling."

"He'll love her," I assured him again, but when I glanced over to him I realized that it wasn't just the car he was talking about.

"Not as much as I do," my dad said, his eyes welling up with tears.

"No," I said, feeling my chest tighten and my throat start to close. "No," I repeated, pointing accusingly at him while trying to focus my attention out of the front windshield so I wouldn't miss our turn. "You are not allowed to make me cry. This is a happy trip." After finding the road and making the turn I risked glancing back at my father. "We've cried enough tears haven't we?" I asked, sniffling back my own tears.

My father cleared his throat. "That we have. That we have." I turned into the driveway but instead of parking in front of the garage next to the other cars I'd prearranged with Mr. Ronson a few houses down from the house to use his driveway so Preppy wouldn't see his surprise before it was time. My stomach flipped wondering what his response would be.

"He's not like other guys," I explained to my dad for the seventh time since we've been in the car together. Earlier Ray and I picked him up at the airport in King's truck before she dropped both of us off at the auto-transport center to receive the car and make sure it survived the journey. I had held my breath through the entire inspection, but luckily, she was good to go.

I went to grab my dad's bag from the trunk but he stopped me. "I'm staying with an old friend in town. No need to take that out. I'll pull it out when I call for a cab later."

"What friend?" I asked, he hadn't mentioned a single thing in the weeks leading up to his visit. I'd always just assumed he'd stay with us.

He switched the subject and led me away from the car before I could ask him more about this mystery friend. "And don't you worry about what I'm going to think of him. You'll remember that I have spoken to him a couple of times before so I have a little idea."

You have no fucking idea.

"Yes, but those weren't good conversations. I just, I don't want you to hate him. It's important to me."

"Darling," he said, wrapping his arm around my shoulder and pulling me in close as we made our way over to the gate. "I'm your dad," he lowered his voice to a whisper when we heard the partygoers in the backyard and saw the flame of the bonfire. "It's my duty to hate whoever you choose to love. But," he flashed me a big smile. "You're not exactly like other young women so why would I expect you to be with a man like all the others? Have you seen that dating show? The Single Man? Honestly if that's what the young men of today behave like then I'm glad you like this man who …how does the saying go? Likes to beat hard on his own drum."

I chuckled at his total failure to say 'Beat of his own drum', but when it came to Preppy, beat his own drum hard worked just as well. "Yeah, Dad. Something like that. And…" I paused and turned to him. "Just…thank you. For everything," I said in an almost whisper. "I don't deserve a dad as great as you."

"Yes, you do," he argued as we started walking again. You deserve the world."

"One more thing," he said, pointing his finger in the air as the thought came to him.

"What?" I asked, a knee jerk sense of dread hit me instantly.

My dad contorted his face. "Do I have to call him Preppy?" And with that the dread cleared and we made our way into the party, arm and arm, laughing.

I never answered him.

Ray and Thia were already sitting around the fire talking. I introduced my dad to both of them and then to Billy who got my dad talking about saltwater fishing in no time. While they chatted I scanned the yard for Preppy who was in the corner talking with King and Bear. Their voices traveled as they all spoke excitedly.

"You were there dammit!" Bear yelled, pacing back and forth. Preppy covered his mouth with his hand like he was stifling a laugh. "You talked to me every single day. You were like my…my voice of reason or some shit like that."

"Do you know how fucking stupid that sounds, Bear?" Preppy asked. "I mean, let's put aside your delusion that you heard me talking inside your big head when you thought I was dead…" he raised his arm above his head and pointed down to himself. "…And let's focus on what the fuck you were smoking that made you think that THIS GUY RIGHT HERE could ever be your voice of fucking reason?"

Bear tugged at his hair and growled. "Fuck it, I give up on life, man."

"Good call. Because seriously, you're sucking at it," Preppy said, followed by King's deep bellowing laugh and a groan from Bear.

As if he sensed me looking at him he turned around. When our eyes met his smile only grew brighter. He jogged across the yard and lifted me up into his arms. "I have a surprise for you," I murmured into his ear.

"Anal?" he shouted the question. The yard grew silent and the dozen or so party goers turned their attention to us, including my dad who cleared his throat.

"Prep?" I asked, he still hadn't let me down and was snuggling his nose into my hair.

"This is my dad," I said. Preppy let finally let me go and in the most Preppy move ever he also seemed to give no shits that he just shouted the word ANAL in front of my father who he was meeting for the first time.

"Hi Mr. Capulet. I'm Samuel Clearwater," Preppy announced happily, "I've thought about this moment a lot and I wanted to let you know that I will take no less than three furlongs of land and seven of your finest milking goats. That's my final offer, Sir." Then, without missing a beat he ignored my father's still extended hand and wrapped him in a tight hug without moving me out of the way first. Therefore, I became the meat in a hug sandwich between my two favorite men in the entire world.

I also couldn't breathe.

I'd never been happier.

"Excuse me, son?" my dad asked after Preppy finally let us go. Well, let my dad go. I was still plastered to his side. His arm around my waist, his fingers dancing on my hip.

Still.

Never happier.

"I thought that's how this whole thing works? First the men negotiate. That's how they do it in the movies. Although we are doing it a little backwards so I can understand the confusion," Preppy deadpanned.

"What the fuck kind of movies are you watching?" I asked, not even caring that I just swore in front of my father who was staring at Preppy as if he just sprouted another head from his neck. I couldn't NOT smile up at him and his craziness. "Furlongs? Goats?"

Preppy shrugged, "I don't know, Doc, the kind where farm animals and land are exchanged before shit like this goes down. Maybe it was the Princess Bride…" he wondered, looking off to the bay for a beat before focusing his smile back on my dad whose eyebrows were drawn in so tight they made a V down the middle of his forehead so sharp I thought it might slice his face in two.

"Wait, how what shit works?" my dad asked, using a rare swear word of his own. "What are we talking about here?"

Preppy released me temporarily to step over to the mismatched coolers on the grass against the back porch. He tossed a beer to my dad who caught it and immediately popped the top. Preppy pulled out two more, opening both of them before handing one to me. "Well, I suppose I could settle for one less furlong of land. I tell you what, sir, as soon as I figure out how much a furlong of land is, I'll get back to you with my new terms. Sound good?" Preppy asked, taking a sip of his beer.

My father sighed, and I tried my hardest not to laugh knowing full well what it's like to meet Preppy for the first time. "Son, you either need to tell me what you're talking about or up your medication, because I'm an old man and you've got me spinning in circles over here and I've only had a sip of beer." He looked at me. "Do you know what he's talking about?" I shook my head because honestly I had no idea, but I knew there was a point, there was always a point.

Well, *sometimes* there was a point.

My dad took another swig of his beer and I did the same, the cool bubbles tickling my tongue and throat. Of course it just so happens that Preppy waited until my father and myself had a mouthful of beer to explain himself, which resulted in the two of us spraying beer out of our mouths and noses.

On ourselves.

On each other. And to the delight of others, on everyone within a three feet radius.

"Doc's dowry of course," Preppy explained like we should have already known. "You know, for your daughter's hand in marriage."

"Am I cattle?" I asked.

"I don't know? Do you want to be?" Preppy asked, waggling his eyebrows.

"I don't even know what that means!" I laughed, swatting him on the shoulder.

"Ahem," my dad said, shaking his empty beer bottle. "I think I'm going to need another one of these before this conversation goes any further."

Preppy jogged off to get him another one as Bo came crashing into my leg. Max and Sammy had been chasing him around the yard. My father didn't miss a beat. "Is this the famous Bo?" he asked, crouching down.

Bo hid behind my leg.

"He's a little shy," I explained to my father. I reached around to give Bo's hair a rustle. "Bo this is your..." I paused, not knowing what my dad wanted to be called. Thankfully he finished for me.

My father waved me off. "Bo I'm your Grandpa. You can call me Grandpa or Papa or…" I gave my dad a stern look to remind him that Bo didn't talk. "You can call me whatever you would like." Dad took his open hand and held his thumb to his forehead. Bo peered out from behind me. When Dad was sure Bo was looking he moved his hand away from his face making two small arches in the air. "That's the hand sign for Grandpa."

My heart melted and I felt like I was going to cry. "What the heck's wrong with you?"

"I have something in my eye!" I snapped, and my father just laughed. Bo pointed up at me and smiled at his new grandpa. "Oh great, you're making fun of me too!" I said, reaching around to tickle him.

"I have something for you, Bo," my dad said. Preppy came around then with my dad's beer in hand. Dad opened his wallet. Your mom says you're six years old which means I owe you six years worth of birthday, Christmas, easter…" he counted out several bills before taking everything from his wallet and pushing it into Bo's hands.

"Dad you don't have to do that, especially since…" I started but stopped not wanting to bring up my dad losing his store and damage his pride.

"Especially since what? You can say it dear," Dad said, standing up. Preppy knelt and helped a smiling Bo count his money.

"Especially since you LOST your business," I said in a low voice.

Dad surprised me by laughing. Preppy picked up Bo and placed him on his shoulders, hanging onto his knees. Bo wrapped his little arms around Preppy's head, covering his eyes with his hands. Preppy lifted them so he could exchange a knowing glance with my father.

"What's going on here?" I asked. "What am I missing?"

"Your dad didn't lose his store," Preppy said.

"He didn't?"

Dad shook his head. "Nope. I was bought out. Some big bookstore made me a more than fair offer and I jumped on it. They don't even want to take it over, they just paid me to close up and get out of the way. Either way, now I'm debt free and my schedule has been cleared up to spend more time with my beautiful daughter and her new family."

"And you knew about this?" I asked Preppy who was leaning to one side as far as he could without Bo falling off.

"Maybe?" he said, but it came out like a question. He set Bo down on the grass and the two of them took off across the yard, chasing one another through the small crowds of people who happily made way for the new father and son.

"Us boys. We chatted," Dad said, slyly.

"When?" I asked.

"The day you came back from Logan's Beach…and every other day since," Dad said. He pointed to Preppy who caught Bo in his arms and was twirling him around, his feet barely missing King and Bear who jumped back and pretended to have been hit. "That Samuel. I don't know what to make of him. Frankly I don't understand half the shit that comes out of his mouth, but I know one thing and it's the only thing that matters in my book."

"What's that?"

"That he loves you. He looks at you the same way I looked at your mom, but I didn't need to see it to know it. I heard it in his voice long before that," my dad said, wrapping his arms around my shoulders.

I wiped my eyes, sniffling.

"No more tears, kid," my dad said with a laugh. "This is a time to celebrate!"

"Wait," I said, realizing something. "So between their money and the money from the sale of Mirna's house, you'll be okay, then? At least for awhile I mean?"

My dad nodded and took a swig of his beer. "Kid, your old man will be set until Bo there is ready to go to college. And that's just with the money from the store sale. I never touched the money you put in my account from Mirna's house. I transferred it right back down here into an account in Bo's name. You can use it for his college or whatever else he'll need growing up. Trust me, kids are expensive," he said with a smile. Dad gave my shoulder another squeeze. "I'm going to go find the little boys room."

I watched him walk toward the house. I pulled at my imaginary sleeves. Preppy came up beside me and put his hands on his knees. He was out of breath from running around with Bo who was now happily chasing Max and Sammy around the yard.

I pressed my lips together, trying not to laugh. "I'm not out of breath, your out of breath," he said, standing upright and pulling me against his chest. He gave me a quick peck on the cheek and was off again, heading toward all three kids making monster noises.

"Penny for your thoughts?" Ray asked, sauntering over with one hand in her back pocket and a beer in the other.

"My dad, he never used the money from the sale of Mirna's house," I said, still not quite able to believe what he just told me. "The money, he put it in an account for Bo."

"I know," Ray said.

"I'm happy he did it, but I wish we would have known sooner. Wait, you know..."

"Yeah, I know," she admitted. "Sooner when? Like before you sold the house?"

"Yeah," I agreed, more confused than ever. "But oh well, I guess things happen for a reason. I mean, I can't believe my dad got such a great offer on the store when it was failing so miserably. Whether they only paid him to close or not it seems odd that a company would pay so much money for a failing business."

"It is odd, because it never happened."

"Huh?"

Ray rocked back on her feet. My dad came out of the house and I officially introduced him to Ray. "Mr. Capulet, Dre was just telling me about the sale of your business, congratulations. Tell me, do you remember the name of the company that bought your store?" she asked, chewing on her lip.

My dad looked up and twisted his lips. "Let me think. Oh yeah, now I remember. Bow Tied Books." He pointed to Preppy. "Fitting isn't it?" he asked, not making the same connection I had.

I spit out my beer and Ray chuckled.

"You okay?" my dad asked.

"Yeah, this beer is skunked. That's all."

One of the GG's came over to introduce themselves to my dad. "Told you so," Ray sang in my ear. "And here, these belong to you," she said, tossing me a set of keys that I recognized them instantly by Mirna's green lucky rabbit foot keychain. "I already signed it back over to both you and Preppy."

"How?" I asked.

Ray shrugged. "It's a long story."

"I'll pay you back. I'll…"

"No," Ray said, closing my hand around the keys. "This is what family does." She looked over to Preppy who now had Bo on his back and were chasing King and Sammy while Max shrieked around them, hiding behind Bear's legs. "And like it or not, you're family now." And with that Ray sauntered over to King and stood on her tip-toes, planting a small kiss on his mouth. He returned her kiss with one of his own that wasn't nearly as PG.

"Dre, do you know if there is any wine around?" My dad asked. "Sandra isn't such a big fan of beer."

I smiled at the grey haired lady my father had his arm linked with. "I'm on it. I think there is a bottle of red inside." I ran up the porch and it only took me a minute to find a bottle of wine which had dust on it. I was trying to find a wine opener when I realized that it was a screw cap. "Hopefully Sandra doesn't mind old cheap red," I said to myself.

With a beer bottle in hand I turned around and stopped just short of crashing into Bo who had a frown on his face where only moments before he was smiling from ear to ear.

"Hey Bo! What's the matter?" I asked, crouching down and inspecting him for any play session injuries. He vigorously shook his head from side to side. He looked up at me and his eyes went wide. Sheer terror was written all over his perfect baby face. When I realized it wasn't me he was looking at, but something over my shoulder, it was already too late.

I was already too late.

A strong hand holding a rag came over my nose and mouth, the other gripping the back of my neck. Before I could even think to fight off whatever or whoever was behind me, my limbs went numb. My brain floated around in my skull. Bo's frightened image turned blurry, and then sideways as I crashed to the floor.

My heart broke. Bo was scared I couldn't help him. I couldn't protect him. Only a few days in and I'd already failed him as his mother. As the blackness claimed me I heard a strangled cry. A beautiful yet painful sound. I drifted off into somewhere unfamiliar, grateful that the last thing I might ever hear was my son's little voice for the very first time.

Even though he was screaming.

"Mooooooooommmmmmmmy!"

The End (for now)

PREPPY,
THE LIFE AND DEATH OF
SAMUEL CLEARWTER,
PART THREE

COMING SOON

More Books By T.M. Frazier

KING SERIES:

KING

TYRANT

LAWLESS

SOULLESS

PREPPY, PART ONE

STANDALONES:

THE DARK LIGHT OF DAY, A KING SERIES PREQUEL

ALL THE RAGE, A KING SERIES SPIN OFF

ABOUT THE AUTHOR

T.M. Frazier is a ***USA TODAY*** BESTSELLING AUTHOR best known for her ***KING SERIES***. She was born on Long Island, NY. When she was eight years old she moved with her mom, dad, and older sister to sunny Southwest Florida where she still lives today with her husband and daughter.

When she was in middle school she was in a club called AUTHORS CLUB with a group of other young girls interested in creative writing. Little did she know that years later life would come full circle.

After graduating high school, she attended Florida Gulf Coast University and had every intention of becoming a news reporter when she got sucked into real estate where she worked in sales for over ten years.

Throughout the years T.M. never gave up the dream of writing and with her husband's encouragement, and a lot of sleepless nights, she realized her dream and released her first novel, The Dark Light of Day, in 2013.

She's never looked back.

For more information on her books and
appearances please visit her website

www.tmfrazierbooks.com

FOLLOW T.M. FRAZIER ON SOCIAL MEDIA

FACEBOOK: www.facebook.com/tmfrazierbooks
INSTAGRAM: www.instagram.com/t.m.frazier
TWITTER: www.twitter.com/tm_frazier

For business inquiries please contact Kimberly Brower
of Brower Literary & Management.
www.browerliterary.com

CPSIA information can be obtained
at www.ICGtesting.com
Printed in the USA
LVOW11s1611140217
524243LV00001BA/216/P